Painting Pictures

Painting Pictures
and other stories

Gayle Gonsalves

INSOMNIAC PRESS

Copyright © 2013 by Gayle Gonsalves

All rights reserved. No part of this publication may be reproduced, stored in a retrieval system or transmitted, in any form or by any means, without the prior written permission of the publisher or, in the case of photocopying or other reprographic copying, a licence from Access Copyright, 1 Yonge Street, Suite 1900, Toronto, ON M5E 1E5

Library and Archives Canada Cataloguing in Publication

Gonsalves, Gayle, 1963-, author
Painting pictures and other stories / Gayle Gonsalves.

ISBN 978-1-55483-113-5 (pbk.)

I. Title.

PS8613.O545P33 2013   C813'.6   C2013-906556-3

The publisher gratefully acknowledges the support of the Canada Council, the Ontario Arts Council, and the Department of Canadian Heritage through the Canada Book Fund.

Printed and bound in Canada

Insomniac Press
520 Princess Avenue, London, Ontario, Canada, N6B 2B8
www.insomniacpress.com

  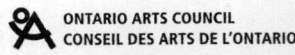

I dedicate this book to my family.
You make life so much nicer.

I have to say a special thank you to Althea Prince for reminding me that I have stories to write. One Sunday morning, her wise brown eyes looked at me and gave me the best advice of my life: "It's time, Gayle." That's when I took up my pen and refound my writing voice. Her encouragement and support was invaluable in this collection.

Thanks to Insomniac Press for reading my work, taking a chance, and publishing this anthology. Your insight and sharp editorial pen has allowed these pages to blossom.

Over the years, I've attended writing groups where I learned to hone my skills. Although I've lost touch with several friends, their constructive advice was truly a blessing as I discovered how to shape a story and use words. There is much gratitude to Brian Mackie and several others.

Thanks to my sister, Nicola, for her intuitive ear—there is no better sister than you; my mom for listening to me read my stories over the phone, so that I could hear how my stories flowed; my brother—thanks for being real; Barbara, for our many phone calls about character and plots; and my dad for being my biggest fan and my rock.

I've been blessed with wonderful family and friends who've been part of my writing life in small and large ways. I truly appreciate your time and support.

Contents

Painting Pictures	11
Clarissa's Letter	31
A Good Woman	43
Caught in a Chasm	65
Jumbies Don't Sleep	77
Secrets Never Shared	89
Tamarind Stew	103
Feel-Good Thing	115

Painting Pictures

I paint pictures. I capture moments on canvas. I convey emotions with the stroke of my brush. Colours create images from my never-ending imagination. My paintings, the receptacles of my thoughts and memories, adorn the walls of my home and are the vehicle through which I communicate.

I've sold paintings to clients all over the world, but I have eight paintings that will never be sold; they will always be mine. At the end of the day, when I am alone in my home with only the sounds of the night for my companion, I'm pulled to the paintings like a lover I can't refuse. When I stand before them, waves of emotions engulf me. I am naked on these walls though I wear clothes. Everything I've done or thought is before me, bold and vibrant. As I look at my life, my breath slows.

I began painting because I was fearful of speaking and found colour and shapes articulated ideas better than I could. Now, as I look at these eight canvases, I realize that my paintings are my words and I've made myself immortal through them.

— Hyatt Walsh

Theo reads the opening paragraphs of the book. His voice slowly caresses each word, and when he finishes, he stares at the page. Because I understand him, I know he is intoxicated by the writer's style. He sits for a moment and closes the book. The bold, purple text of the book's title, *Painting Pictures*, sits inside an ornate frame that decorates the cover. Theo hands me the book and pulls my hand into his with a strong vicelike grip. He always holds my hand with such force, as if claiming me. The first time he touched me in this manner years ago his hold was strong and shocked me because I did not expect it.

"I bought you this book when I was in Japan," he enthusiastically says. "Look." He points to a white sticker in the top corner. "Can you see it? It's the price tag in Japanese. Isn't that neat?"

I smile indulgently at him. "Yes, it is."

"I couldn't believe it when I saw the book on the shelf, and then I opened it and read the remarkable words of this painter. I thought this would be a unique gift for you from Japan," he gushes.

"But this book is on bookshelves here in Toronto," I quietly reply.

"I know, but do you know anyone who has a copy from Japan?"

"No."

"Now you do, and the price tag authenticates it. Here you go. You are the proud owner of this book that was bought halfway around the world."

"Why this book?"

He flips it over, and I see the smiling face of the author staring at me; Theo's patriotic side emerges.

"Look at the author. She's from the same island where you were born. She is us. She's from the Caribbean, and I was so proud to see the words from our little islands travelling so far. And then I realized how much I wished you were with me."

He places the book in my hands. I open it and read his inscription: *To Rena, you continue to intrigue and inspire. T.*

He reaches over and whispers, "It's so good to see you. While I was in Japan, you were away. How was your holiday? Did you miss me?"

I smile as I softly touch his arms. "I had a great time in Antigua. It always brings me back to my centre. And, yes, you know I miss you when you're not with me. I thought about you quite a lot."

"One day we should go to Antigua together. I'd love to see your skin glistening in the sea," he replies as he gently nibbles on my neck. "And perhaps we can go to Hyatt Walsh's studio and look at her art."

In the background, there is the unmistakable, heavy sound of a train pulling into the station. Although the building is sound, it shakes slightly with its movement. All around us people are running to catch a train, but we are cordoned off from the bustle, sitting in a hidden nook, a place that gives us privacy.

Theo looks at his watch. "I've got to run, but I'll call you later. I don't want to miss my train."

He brushes my lips and leaves. I am now alone at a busy train station with a book in my lap. I look at the cover and flip to the back to see the smiling eyes of the author, Hyatt Walsh. The contours of her face and the copper colour of her skin tell the story of her mixed origin. She is a true Caribbean pepper pot; her face contains an identity carved from the different peoples who live in this region. I know her face. I understand the shape of her lips and the curl of her hair; they are very similar to mine. We are blood. Theo doesn't know that she and I are family.

Hyatt Walsh is my aunt—my mother's half-sister, my grandfather's love child. My mother's mouth always curled at the side whenever she spoke of her sibling. She always referred to her as "Hyatt, my father's outside child" to ensure that everyone knew that they didn't share the same maternal bloodline. My mother only saw her sister as tainted by the status of illegitimacy, despite Hyatt's status as the Caribbean's most celebrated painter and author. As I look at my aunt's face, I can picture Theo's excitement to see a book written by a Caribbean person prominently displayed in a bookstore halfway around the world. I know he instinctively picked it up thinking that I'll really enjoy it, wholly unaware of the connection. Although my aunt is now in her sixties, I smile as I remember her. We have always been close. When I was a youngster, I spent many afternoons with her, and now that I am an adult, no trip home is complete without spending copious amounts of time with her. As a child, she ignored my other siblings and cousins and took me into her studio to teach me about colour. She noted my artistic eye and wanted to school me about the world of shapes, undertones, and lighting. My mother, a lawyer, was uncomfortable with my artistic nature and tried to keep me focused on a traditional educational route; she didn't want me meandering on the same path as her father's outside child, whose free-spirited lifestyle was the cause for much gossip on the small island.

When my mother forbade me from visiting my aunt at her studio because she thought it was a waste of time, it was Hyatt who interceded. I remember her storming into our home and yelling at my mother, "Catherine, you can't make that child into your image. She is different to you; she's creative. Let her become who she is meant to be."

My mother looked angrily at her. "What do you know about bringing up a child? If I remember correctly, you can't bear one."

For a moment, my aunt's face looked pained, but she quickly regained her composure. "I may never be able to have a child, but I know when you're hurting one."

Although my mother didn't want me to follow in her father's outside child's image, she reluctantly agreed to allow me to spend time with her. I whiled away many hours in Aunt Hyatt's art studio and learned how to draw. Although I am an excellent artist, I didn't become a painter. Nor did my life path lead me to law. I followed my creative desires and became a graphic designer.

My mother thought, and she still believes, that the

only real art was created outside of the Caribbean. My childhood home was adorned with Monet prints and large Spanish paintings filled with bullfighters, but never anything tropical. And there was nothing on the walls that was created by her respected father's outside child or even her daughter who was renowned for creating beautiful watercolours.

The two sisters are four years apart, and I believe my mother hated her sister for many reasons. Part of her disliked that Hyatt represented her father's love for another woman who was not her mother, and another side of my mother hated that her childhood dream died when she learned that she was not her father's only treasured daughter, and he'd been lying to her. Until they met in their twenties, the two sisters lived on the same island but were unaware of their paternal bond.

It was through their love for me that they brokered a peace that grew into a grudging acceptance, and, with time, they called each other every now and then to say hello. Despite their very different professional choices, they were both their father's daughters and carried many of his traits; each was a hard-working and successful woman in her chosen career, and through their forced friendship, they acknowledged their respect for each other. And, despite their different mothers, they both looked very much alike; fate played a dirty trick on my grandfather and he could not hide his secret because the girls were identical in face.

Theo doesn't know any of this. He doesn't know that I've watched my aunt work with a white apron that was splattered with thousands of paint spots. And he doesn't know that she loved painting me or that my childish face can be found in many of her paintings.

As I flip through her book, I come to a section that reminds me of some of the words that she and I have shared.

Like any artist, I create from a blank canvas. My days and nights are spent applying layer after layer of paint, manipulating a brush, creating an image. I've poured my soul into my paintings, and I get attached to them like a mother to a child. And it tears my soul when they leave my studio for another wall. There are times when I've cried for days because, like a mother whose baby was torn from her, I suffer deeply. That is why I will never part with my eight self-portraits—they are my children.

As I've always been one of her favourite subjects to paint, she always insists on painting my portrait whenever I return to the island. Although I've tried to back out a few times, she finds a way to coerce me to sit still for hours. Her paintings are like my pictorial diary since they capture me from childhood to the present day. She once told me, "Rena, I love painting you because you never hold anything back. Your whole life is on your face."

Only my free-spirited aunt knows about Theo. On my recent visit to Antigua, I spent many afternoons with her so that she could paint me. There, in her beautiful home that overlooks the Caribbean Sea, I sat in a chair next to a bright red hibiscus tree. On the first day when I relaxed into the chair, she stood at a distance and looked at me for a long time; then she came closer and quietly smiled. She returned to her easel and said, "I see you have colour again." That was when I told her about Theo.

I met Theo while standing in line buying coffee, but his version of our first encounter is vastly different than mine. He agrees that it was a Wednesday in the middle of summer, and it happened at Union Station as we made our way home from our offices in different high-rise buildings in downtown Toronto. The train station was filled with the usual flurry of rush hour madness as people moved quickly along the well-worn floors to catch their trains; they instinctively climbed stairs and rapidly scurried about, immune to the sweet sugary scents that wafted through the air.

Before we met, I was standing in a line to purchase tickets for my commute. According to Theo, we met in this lineup, even though I never saw or spoke to him. This is his version of our meeting. He was standing in line cursing himself for not buying his tickets at lunchtime to avoid the crowd, because he hated lines, then he smelled the sweet scent of coconut oil and his anger quickly dissipated. His attention was diverted. He had a flashback to his childhood when he saw an old man with very grey hair tenuously scale the slender trunk of a coconut tree. On his way up, the man's concerned wife kept telling him to come down because he was too old to be climbing. But he ignored her pleas; he was intent on climbing the tree. Once he reached the top, the man screamed with joy and gleefully threw the coconuts to the ground. There was a joyous, loud thump when each oval hit the earth.

Theo looked around wondering where the smell came from and realized the stranger standing in from of him was the source of the familiar scent. He then noted that my curly ringlets ended just below my shoulder and immediately held back his instinct to touch their swirl. Even today, after two years together, when he plays with my hair, he will ravel a strand around his fingers, letting it twirl around him, always fascinated that it could so easily twist into him. He laughs and says, "They are like friendly, playful handcuffs."

But on that day, before I met him, he stood behind me, fighting his desire to touch my hair. He noticed that I was wearing a pink jacket that nipped at my waist and my skirt flared at my bottom. He quietly smiled as he imagined grabbing its roundness.

The line moved quickly, and I was no longer standing in front of him. Once he bought his ticket, he acknowledged his curiosity was piqued and knew he wanted to see my face; that was why, after he bought his ticket, he followed me to the coffee shop. He told himself that once he saw what I looked like, he'd let it go.

I thought it was a coincidence when a strange man with a Caribbean accent came to my rescue when I was two dollars short of the money needed to purchase a cup of coffee and a muffin. I heard a voice saying, "It's okay; I'll make up the difference," and I turned around to see the smiling face of a man who seemed very amused by my predicament.

His eyes were a deep brown, like the earth after the rain, and his skin had a rich mocha smoothness that made his smile shine. As his hand placed the money in the sales clerk's hand, I grabbed the coffee. He chuckled as we walked away.

"I didn't realize I spent most of my money buying my monthly pass; that's why I was short of cash," I clumsily explained as we left the shop. "Give me your number and I'll arrange to pay you back."

He laughed heartily. "It's only a toonie. I won't go broke if I give that away. Forget about it; it's nothing."

"Yeah, you're right, but this was really quite embarrassing. Thanks for helping me out."

"Seeing you smile is enough. Where are you from?" he asked. "I hear an island accent, but I'm not sure which island you're from."

"Antigua," I said, "and what about you? I know you're also from the Caribbean."

"St. Lucia, home of the Pitons. By the way, my name is Theo. I have an idea: why don't you talk to me for repayment?"

"Two dollars doesn't get you a lot of time," I coyly replied.

"Depends on where you are in the world. For a farmer

in Zimbabwe, it's a day's salary—that's around ten hours. They work long days there. You may be stuck with me for quite some time."

My train was delayed while his train was on time, but he didn't take it. I said nothing as he led me to a quiet corner. Forty minutes later, my train was sitting on its track; it was time to leave.

"Can we have lunch tomorrow?" he asked as I bid him farewell.

"I guess I still owe you a few hours," I laughed as I gave him my number.

The next day, we ate together. And the following day, we went to a hotel. We entered an impeccably furnished hotel suite with a plush bed with rings on our fingers, but we took them off and rested them on the dresser. They didn't match: mine was a diamond solitaire that my husband saved earnestly for many months to afford, while Theo's was a plain platinum band.

I was bashful when Theo first touched me, and my shyness shocked him. It surprised me, too. I'd made love hundreds of times.

"I've been with my husband for so long that I've forgotten what it's like to be with someone else," I confided. I didn't look into his eyes as I spoke. It was as if this was a tragic statement.

Theo stopped kissing me. "Are you sure you want to do this?"

"My husband and I haven't had sex in over two years."

He pulled away from me, and I wasn't sure if he

wanted to continue. I knew he was thinking that this could be more trouble than he'd anticipated. But his hands were playing with my hair; my ringlets were cuffed around his fingers.

"It's your hair," he exclaimed. "That's what smells so good." And then he pulled me to him.

He took the eastbound train; I took the westbound train. Our lives intersected at Union Station. We were like millions of nameless commuters in big cities—small dots moving quickly and quietly to their destinations. The inbound trains took us to our respective offices that were filled with people, strangers who saw a minute slice of us. These were some of the people for whom we painted a picture that our marriages were perfect, with whom we spoke of our busy weekends cleaning large homes and socializing with friends, lying about the intimacies that didn't happen in our bedrooms over the weekend; they never really heard the true colours behind our words.

Our affair was discreet. We believed no one noticed. Who cares about middle-aged people having an affair? To the world, we were two mature adults, still laughing together after many years of monogamy; they didn't notice that we weren't wearing matching rings. People have an insatiable interest in the youth and their instability of mind, so they don't stop to notice an affair between two mature people. I guess it's because they think that passion is finite and not part of your entire lifetime; they've forgotten that we can always remake our lives the way we remake our bed each day.

Because I am like my aunt and I see life through colour and form, I knew I could always draw a new picture, but the truth was that for a long time I was hesitant to pick up my sketch pad. Before Theo, I accepted that I was a forty-something-year-old woman, not yet menopausal but with waning desires. My life felt like a small closet in an old house without light or shelves. As a mother, I watched my daughter become a young woman, and I saw there wasn't a mirror that could give our faces the same youthful reflection, despite our obvious physical resemblance. I didn't cry for those lost years, but I often wondered, "Where did they go?" After Theo, I quickly learned that there is no line between young and old; it was just one colour with varying shades of light and dark. There was nothing rational about my actions, and I didn't care that I could hurt myself or that I could also hurt someone else. I only knew that each day, I became aware that I could draw beautiful sketches again and add colour to them. That was when I realized that life is a line—one with a beginning and an ending. What you do to that line to keep it from becoming straight and colourless is what matters.

For two years, Theo and I met at Union Station; his train arrived five minutes before mine, and he'd wait patiently for me at the coffee shop. We'd sit together, and he'd take my hand in his. Our eyes were always alight as we sipped our morning brew and exchanged words before we went to our various offices. Theo travelled frequently in his job, and this allowed us special privileges in a variety of hotel rooms in the city.

I didn't want our affair to unravel. I waited every morning for him, knowing that one morning, I could step off the train and he wouldn't be there. And I could never call.

During my recent trip to Antigua, each morning I'd go to the sea, then I'd make my way to Aunt Hyatt's home and sit for several hours while she painted me.

On my final day, my aunt presented me with a canvas. I looked at it in amazement because she'd captured Theo as a shadow in the background.

She smiled and said, "I'm not judging you, Rena, and I promise I never will. Enjoy him, Rena; you deserve it after all you've put up with from your wutless husband. My sweet niece, treasure the colour while it is there. It only takes the wrong stroke of a paintbrush to wipe it out."

Her book sits on my lap. I look at my watch: it is time to catch my train and go home to the suburbs where I live my life of quiet pretense with a husband who sleeps in another room. I remember that day, several years ago, when I told my aunt why I cast him out of my room. Once again, I was sitting on her balcony that overlooked the Caribbean Sea, and she was painting me, immortalizing those emotions on canvas. At that time, I was stunned to see the painting was devoid of colour; even the red hibiscus tree had no bloom. My aunt, who was known for her love of bright, bold colours, painted that portrait sterile: black and white. I returned to Toronto and hung that picture in my bedroom, where I spent many hours inspecting it, hoping that it'd answer my questions about my decision to tell the man I'd spent twenty years with to vacate our bedroom. Once, my husband ventured into the room, hoping to beg me to change my mind. But when he saw the picture, he stared at it for a few moments, then he turned around and left. Although the painting is not my aunt's signature style, I love it because its scarcity of colour digs so deep into my psyche that it screams my pain.

As I sit on the train and look out the window, the cityscape disappears and a suburban landscape, with its dots of boxlike houses, becomes the scenery. I remember Aunt Hyatt once allowed me into her secret room, where I was finally able to see her eight self-portraits. As I stood, amazed by the sheer size and complexity of the paintings, she said, "Don't ever stay too long in something that makes you forget about colour. It's horrible how we can let someone make us forget how vibrant life can be. Look at my paintings. Look at these eight self-portraits that I painted. I know you understand what they say, and can tell when colour returned to my life."

Finally, the train ride is over and I am in the suburbs. I get into my car and drive home. When I reach the house,

I go directly to my bedroom, and I stare at the sterile, angry painting for a long time. Then I remove the canvas from the wall. I place it next to the new painting that I've placed in the corner. I compare the two paintings.

What no one knows is what my aunt's wonderful eight paintings tell about her. There is one that shows her tears when she said her final goodbye to her father at his funeral, and another when she mourned the disappointment of losing her first love; one of them shows her celebrating her creativity with a wild dance, and there is a painting where she holds her belly and cries because her womb cannot bear children. Her self-portraits are her diaries, and each stroke of her brush speaks of her pain and her understanding of her losses. And because of our bond, she immortalizes my face to tell my story. I look at the two pictures she painted of me. I trace the contours and strokes of her brush that so vividly captures the duality of colour and colourlessness. Finally, I put the picture of my suffering face in the cupboard and place my new colourful one on the wall.

As I prepare for bed, I know that tomorrow morning I will take the train to Union Station, where I'll meet Theo. I will sit and have coffee with him before I go to work and design a new brochure for a client. This is my life right now. This is all I can handle. I don't know where it will go.

And I know there will be a day when I will journey back to Antigua and my famous aunt will paint another canvas, but I don't know what it'll look like because by that time I'll no longer be sneaking off to plush hotel rooms with Theo.

Clarissa's Letter

"I'm going to see snow," I told my cousins.

"It's just like that white stuff in the freezer," Adrianna exclaimed.

"You're so lucky, Clarissa!" Ashton, Adrianna's brother, added.

We knew little about snow. Our only exposure was pictures and television, but we had spent many long hours, sitting amongst the red hibiscus on my grandmother's veranda, discussing snow, and believing that the most amazing experience in the world would be to touch it. That afternoon signalled the last of those conversations, as I was leaving the following day for a country where it snowed.

My mother and I lived with my grandmother in a green wood house with a colourful garden, lush with bougainvillea and yellow bells, on Antigua, a Caribbean island that boasts 365 breathtaking beaches. My cousins and I were constantly together, either playing at the beach or exploring the rolling hills that surrounded my grandmother's home and getting our feet pricked with cassie bush.

At night, while my mother worked, my grandmother would take a needle and dig the thorns from my feet and tell me stories. She adapted traditional fairy tales to our island setting with local characters and euphemisms. I loved the lilting sound of her voice as it rose and fell to each word in her dulcet Antiguan accent. As she became more engrossed with her storytelling, her dark, wavy hair would gently fall into her face and she'd quietly push those stray strands into her bun.

On my last afternoon, my uncle drove my cousins and me to the beach. Even though I was very familiar with the landscape, I sat quietly in the backseat of my uncle's car and intently observed the brightly coloured homes with pretty gardens and the cows languidly walking on the road. My eyes took in the flowers, the sky, and the countryside and imprinted them into my memory. When I heard the sound of the waves, I inhaled the refreshing sea breeze and quietly held back my tears.

Once my uncle had parked his car, my cousins and I continued our ritual of racing each other to the sea. At nine years of age, I was the smallest and slowest and always the last to jump in, but no one cared. Our laughter rose above the waves as we frolicked in the water and played tag. When our fingers became too wrinkled from the sea, we ran to the shore and played in the sand, where I built a grand sandcastle replete with a moat and drawbridge.

I was on the shore when I heard my uncle telling us it was time to go. Without thinking, I ran back into the sea and splashed the water high into the air, where it quickly rose into the sky and rained on me. I laughed with joy as the cool cascading water hit my skin. Suddenly, I stopped moving and looked at the shoreline; then I turned around and saw the horizon, where the water and sky met in a seamless sapphire line. It was so blue that, even as a child, its beauty subdued me. I was only aware of the sounds of the waves breaking, and it was as if the sound echoed inside me. I wanted to stay here. My uncle called again. My cousins also stood at the shoreline screaming my name, and before I took my final step out of the sea, I closed my eyes and glued this scene into my memory.

I dangled my feet over the gallery, but they didn't touch the ground. Below me the ants prodded through the dirt. They looked as if they were in another universe as their busy bodies moved to and fro in their ant world. My cousins sat next to me. Their feet also dangled over the concrete wall and didn't touch the ground. We were not speaking; they were upset because I kept boasting that I would see snow, and when they told me to stop, I continued.

As we sat on the veranda, we saw a dust cloud in the horizon, and then we heard the crisp sound of tires threading the gravel road. When the car stopped in front of my grandmother's house, we knew it was time for me to leave. I looked at my cousins to say bye, but they stared blankly at me. My eyes pleaded with them because I didn't want to leave with this friction between us. They didn't look at me and just walked away. Before I could say sorry, I was sitting in the car and on my way to the airport.

My grandmother saw my despair and pulled me into her warm, comforting arms. She realized that my cousins and I were fighting and instinctively knew I needed her. Those arms held me at birth; it wasn't until that moment that I realized I was leaving her for another country. I had always assumed that I could climb into her lap. Suddenly, I was scared about my new life without her. As we drove to the airport, I clung to her. While she comforted me, she reminded me that I would be experiencing a different world filled with new adventures. She told me I would have the opportunity to make something of myself because if I did well in school, I could go to university and make her very proud. She also reassured me that my rift with my cousins would mend itself. I believed her because she was always right.

Although the airport was a bevy of activity with people and suitcases, all I remember is sitting in the restaurant next to my mother and grandmother, who were sharing a "sweet" drink. By that time, I had regained my composure and was only thinking about seeing snow. The women were both silent as their eyes shifted around the room observing everything and avoiding each other.

When the loudspeaker announced our flight was boarding, I quickly jumped to my feet. My grandmother smiled indulgently when she saw my impatience. As I hurriedly kissed her goodbye, she pulled me to her and held me so hard that it felt as if she would squeeze all the air out of me. For a moment, I wasn't sure if I could leave her. My mother got up and stood next to my grandmother.

They resembled each other in so many ways from their hand gestures to the brown hue of their skin. As their bright dresses blew buoyantly in the breeze and swung around their legs, they looked at each other. Their eyes were belying an emotion that both couldn't voice. I got tired of their staring at each other and tugged my mother's hand, but she ignored me as she and my grandmother continued looking at each other. Another announcement came over the speaker. We had to leave; time was running out. My mother hugged my grandmother; and, without looking back, she hurriedly grabbed my hand. She walked fast, and I had to scramble to keep up with her. In my excitement, I was unable to understand the tears that fell from my mother's eyes, and I didn't look back to see those that also fell from my grandmother's eyes.

The welcoming face of the attendant greeted me as I was about to enter the plane, but before I stepped through the door, I instinctively turned around one last time. My last vision was the palm trees swaying in the breeze and the deep blue sky that touched eternity.

"Where's the snow?" I asked in shock when we arrived.

My mother saw my confused expression and said, "It's summer, Clarissa."

"Where did the snow go?"

"Don't worry, Clarissa. It'll snow, but first the weather has to change. It's hot now. When it gets cold, it will snow."

"But I have nothing to tell Adrianna and Ashton."

"Clarissa, you're in a new country; there's lots to tell them before the snow comes."

I thought differently.

Summer in this new country was long days filled with lots and lots of bright sunlight. There were many times when the sun was still shining when I went to bed. I was really bothered that the temperature was the same as Antigua because all I wanted to do was tell my cousins that I'd seen snow. In my new life, there was no backyard and I didn't know anyone. We lived in a small apartment, and the neighbours occasionally said hello. Most importantly, I didn't have a playmate.

The first few weeks were very lonely, and I spent a lot of time watching television and looking at the parking lot filled with oil stains. I missed my grandmother. I missed my cousins. I missed swimming and playing at Fort James. I constantly thought about the green house on Old Runway Road and the hills where I buried treasure with my cousins. Here, I spent the day by myself and did nothing. All I wanted was for the snow to come so that I could write to my cousins.

My mother prepared me for winter by buying a new wardrobe. I now had furry boots that I would wear when it snowed. Each morning, I awoke with the expectation of snow, but it didn't come. I could not write my cousins; there wasn't much to tell them because I had no friends and I was alone most of the time.

The temperature fell and it ushered in a new season. I was awed by the spectacular colours of that first autumn. The leaves turned fiery red and yellow hues, and the earth became a magical gold carpet with specks of orange and red. My mother and I took to walking through parks where we would look at the leaves and marvel at the kaleidoscope of colours. I wanted so desperately to write my cousins about this beautiful season but couldn't. I felt a pang of remorse and sadness because I remembered how much I had bragged about seeing snow and I didn't know how to tell them that I was sorry.

The thermometer continued to dip a few more degrees; I'd feel a chill and shiver. One day when I sighed, a white cloud sat before me. Puzzled, I sighed again and another cloud formed. I sighed all day, wholly intrigued by the small clouds I created.

Despite all these changes, there was no snow and no news for my cousins. My grandmother wrote to us, and my mother filled me in with all the news. How my heart ached when she read those letters! I missed my cousins. I missed my grandmother. My grandmother told my mother she was worried because my cousins had not heard from me. I wanted to write, but it had not snowed. It was then that I began to wish that I had not boasted. I was ashamed that I had bragged that I'd see snow. With each passing day, I realized how much I missed my cousins and grandmother. I had no friends and often stared at the parks wishing my cousins were here to play with me.

Time passed, and I awoke one November morning to a sheet of white. The incredible event had come! As I stared in awe, my mother joined me, and we were silent with wonderment. The world was transformed from a dull, grey landscape into sheet of satin white. Everywhere was white from the branches of the trees that softly held the snow to the rooftops; nothing was left untouched. The ugly parking lot with oil stains was now covered with a fluffy white coating that hid its unsightliness and gave it a sense of sheer serenity. It was as if we were in a new country with a smooth white frosting.

"It's so pretty," she said. "It doesn't look real. It's even prettier than in pictures."

"It's magical, Mommy! It's truly magic."

I donned the boots that had been waiting patiently for this moment and ran down the stairs. When I stepped outside, I was amazed at the stillness of the falling snow; unlike the rain, it made no sound. It fell quietly, disturbing no one, only changing the face of the earth. I stuck out my tongue to taste the snowflakes. To my surprise, it melted when it touched my tongue, and its coolness slid quietly down my throat.

The schoolyard was a frenzy of activity. Snowballs danced menacingly in the air, seeking an intended target. Kids were rolling the snow into balls, not just small ones but larger ones to build snowmen. Those who weren't making snowballs were gliding down the hill with toys of all shapes and sizes, and their laughter rang in the schoolyard.

When I felt a tap on my shoulder, I turned and it was one of the girls in my class. She smiled mischievously and then threw a snowball; it hit my face. At first, I was stunned by its cold sting, but after my initial amazement, I grabbed some snow, packed it into a ball, and ran after her. My laughter joined the others in the schoolyard.

I arrived home later than usual after an afternoon of playing in the snow and making new friends. Tired as I was, I grabbed a pen and paper. I began a letter to my cousins:

Dear Adrianna and Ashton,
It snowed today. There was lots of snow, and it was more beautiful than any picture. I wish you were with me so that we could play in it. Snow is light to feel but cold to touch. However, when you place it in your bare hands, it starts to melt.

There is so much you can do with the snow. You can make snowballs and snowmen. It packs well, and you can build huge balls if you want to. You can even build a snow castle—kind of like the sandcastles we built at Fort James.

You won't believe this, but I made gigantic balls, bigger than a beach ball, by rolling and rolling the snow. That's how you make snowmen. Some kids laid down in it and made angels by flapping their hands. That was so neat to see!

It took me a long time to write because it seemed to take forever to snow. When I first came here, it was hot and I was really lonely without you. I didn't do very much, but I thought about you all the time. I wasn't very nice before I left because I boasted a lot about going away. I'm sorry and I promise never to do that again. I miss you so much. Please write soon.

    Love, Clarissa.

Then I put down my pen, put on my boots, and went outside to play in the snow with my new friends.

A Good Woman

An earlier version of this story was published in *In the Black: New African Canadian Literature* edited by Althea Prince

Seven years ago, Linden hastily packed his belongings and moved to Toronto, a city that is vastly different from his small island Caribbean home, where he thrives in the varying weather patterns. During the frigid winter period, he finds solace in books. And on bright summer days, he makes his way to the shores of Lake Ontario, where its immense, sparkling brilliance reminds him of the Caribbean Sea. He closes his eyes and imagines being on a beach with Sandra. Her mahogany skin glistens in the water, and she delicately picks up a shell from the sand; she smiles as she shows him the perfectly shaped shell. Her beautiful, slender fingers touch his arm, moving with the same grace and tenderness she does when she paints a canvas.

It is through the small island grapevine in Toronto that Linden hears about Auntie Jeannie's illness, and he's desperate to know what's going on. With extreme trepidation he calls Antigua, and Sandra answers the phone. Her voice is still a magical, musical tone, and he can't help but melt as she speaks. For a moment, he drifts into his fantasyland but is pulled back to reality when she tells him if he wants to see his aunt one final time, he'd better come home soon.

"I'll take the first flight I can get," he tells her.

"Good," she says. Then she adds, "You know you can't stay here. Kelvin won't have it."

"No problem," he replies, flustered and embarrassed. "I'll make arrangements for a hotel."

Two weeks later, he's asking her a question that upsets her. "Do you think Kelvin's going to make it to Auntie Jeannie's funeral?"

Sandra turns to Linden as he speaks. He looks into her luminous brown eyes. For a moment, she lets down her defences and returns his gaze. They are alone in her home, surrounded by the bright canvases she paints; no one can disturb them, yet when he reaches for her, she turns away.

"He can't live in the rum shop forever. It'll kill him," Sandra quickly replies. "It must be Auntie Jeannie's death that sent him over the edge."

Shortly after they speak, Sandra leaves Linden and takes a short stroll. She walks for a while and then eventually finds herself on Vivian Richards Street, and she makes her way along the narrow thoroughfare to the rum shop. From the road, she hears dominoes slamming on a table and the boisterous voices of the men as they discuss the "tiefing" or "holiness" of the government. The rusted, worn-out sign, *Rawle's, a p ace for fri nds*, hangs lopsided; one of its screws fell a few years ago. The strong smell of the alcohol repulses her, but she ignores it as she opens the shoddy wooden door that leads to Rawle's. She quickly surveys the room and finds Kelvin in his usual corner spot.

She touches his hand. "Kelvin, come nuh. Tomorrow

we bury Auntie Jeannie, and you need to clean up. You've had enough. It's time to come home."

He looks up from his glass with glazed eyes and slurs, "Ssssssannnnnndraaa, darlllling, me one true love. Me can't leave yyyet. Be a gooood wiiffee and jussssst sit with mm-meee whilllle me goooo have one for de rrrooad."

"Kelvin, the bottle goin' kill you. It's time to stop."

But he ignores her and pours himself a drink. She shakes her head in disgust and leaves him sitting on the hard bar stool.

Sandra walks slowly on the cracked concrete sidewalk, carefully navigating the holes and cracks. The route home is different, as she leaves the familiar streets of her neighbourhood and walks north, past Country Pond and through town until she's in a new area where there are homes with beautiful flowers. Her eyes take everything in. She looks at several houses, and then she stops in front of a quaint green house with a small hedge of yellow bells and a yard filled with pawpaw trees. Her artistic eyes admire its lines and dimensions. And she looks at it for a long time before she makes her long return trek. Once home, she sits on the couch and looks blankly at the walls that are filled with her beautiful artwork. She spends all night looking at them.

On the following day, Sandra dresses in a black frock and attends Auntie Jeannie's funeral with Linden. Her legs shake as she walks next to the casket. She sobs uncontrollably, and

Linden holds her tenderly during the funeral. He's surprised by her grief, but he's acutely aware that Sandra is in a very emotional state. After the funeral, she stares at the walls of the house that are filled with her paintings. He watches her warily as she touches her paintbrush and then violently throws it to the ground.

"Let's get out of here," he says as he tugs her arm, fearful that she could cause some damage. "You need to get away. I've been home for nearly a week and haven't been to the sea. I think it's calling us."

Twenty minutes later, he and Sandra are making their way to Fort James Beach, driving on the island's familiar narrow roads and masterfully swerving potholes. Although neither of them can see the beach, they smell the salt in the air and hear the hypnotic sound of the water breaking at the shore. When they finally see the brilliant aqua waters blend into the horizon, their eyes dance with joy. As soon as he turns off the ignition, Linden hears the car door open, and before he can say anything, he sees Sandra hastily run from the car and spontaneously jump into the water. Her gleeful screams fill the air as her body hits the water. Linden smiles and, instinctively, runs into the water to be with her. On that afternoon, as the clock moves backward and forward, he falls in love with her again. Together they walk on the sand. Sandra picks up shells, and when she sees one that intrigues her, he listens carefully as she talks about its colour and lines. He is comforted that she is still the Sandra he remembers, and he wants so desperately for her to be happy. They leave when the sun sets.

That evening, she doesn't think about her husband who is wasting away at Rawle's. Instead, she returns to her canvas and paints the shell. And she surprises Linden by painting a quaint green house surrounded by yellow bells. He notices that her colours are bright, her colours are vibrant, and she's smiling.

Linden and Kelvin are brothers. When their father was alive, he'd say, "How can two pickney from the same belly be so different?"

Throughout their entire lives, everyone who met them commented on their differences. Kelvin, with his dark, athletic looks, was well known for his wild spirit. He drank, partied, and when he entered a room in a tight T-shirt that accentuated his perfect physique, he'd yell, "Whoa! Whoa! Whoa! Kelvin is here! Bring the rum, bring the Coke. Start the music." Linden, on the other hand, was the epitome of sophistication. Always immaculately dressed, he preferred crisp, well-pressed pinstriped shirts with a starched collar to T-shirts. While his brother enjoyed laughing in a crowd, Linden favoured a good book and didn't waste his time on inane social chatter. Kelvin, the entrepreneur of the two, barely passed school but owned a small business that provided for him and his wife. Linden, the scholar, enjoyed analyzing social behaviour and actions. He pursued postsecondary education and commanded a very decent wage at the bank. Only a year apart, the only thing they had in common was their love for Sandra.

After he finished school, Linden won a scholarship to university and left Antigua for several years. During his absence, his brother shocked his family, friends, and all the gossipers on the island by pursuing and marrying the thoughtful and artistic Sandra. For a short time after he placed the wedding ring on her finger, he quietened down, and those who knew him believed that he'd left his wild ways behind him.

When Linden returned to the island, Kelvin was already spending more time at Rawle's than with his wife. His business was suffering, and he asked his brother to move in with them to help with the bills. Linden agreed. Kelvin was pleased with the arrangement; he felt reassured that his brother would make sure no man was "horning" him. But Kelvin never knew or suspected that Linden was obsessed with Sandra's luminous eyes and deep copper complexion.

Every night, Kelvin kissed his wife delicately on the cheek. "I'm just going up the road with the boys. I'll be home later."

As the door closed behind him, Linden quietly smiled because he was alone with Sandra. There, under the roof they all shared, Linden's infatuation grew into love as he discovered Sandra's calm, creative nature. Each night, out of the corner of his eyes, he watched Sandra with absolute fascination. He loved the way she twisted her hair into a scarf before she began painting. He was wholly intrigued by her slender fingers nimbly working the paintbrush as she created new lines and shapes.

As Kelvin disappeared more and more, Sandra and

Linden spent a lot of time together. Once Kelvin used to go with his wife every Saturday afternoon to the beach, but his brother took his place. Together, Linden and Sandra swam in the crystal clear waters and laughed. He'd watch Sandra scour for shells, and when she found one that met her approval, she'd show it to Linden. Her fingers traced its lines as she told him about its texture, dimension, and colour. He loved getting a glimpse into her world and seeing objects through her eyes.

And one Saturday evening after they returned from the beach, with the sand still clinging to their bodies, Linden gave into his desires and pulled Sandra to him. He kissed her on the lips and was ecstatic when her lips moved with his.

Then she pulled away. "I can't. This isn't right."

"Leave him," Linden pleaded. "Marry me. We can make a life together. He doesn't deserve someone as good as you."

"This is crazy. I'm married to your brother. How did this happen?"

"Stop thinking and let it be."

"Linden, this is madness. Utter madness. I'm married to your brother."

"Sandra, I don't care. He doesn't deserve you. Love has no rules."

"He's not all bad. I know the Kelvin few ever see." She paused. "Rum is not a good thing." And she left the room.

The following night, Linden noticed that Sandra was looking at him through the corner of her eyes and waited impatiently for Kelvin to leave. As soon as he closed the door, Linden pulled her into his arms. This time she didn't protest. Finally, she opened up to Linden.

"This is not easy, you know. I thought about what you said. It's not like I don't have feelings for you. I do." Linden's heart beat fast as she spoke. "If I'd met you before I met Kelvin, this would be so different, but I didn't. You are his brother, and this isn't right."

Linden didn't hear the last part of her sentence, and he responded impulsively, "Let's go away together. My papers for Canada just came in. Join me. Divorce him and marry me. I promise that I'll honour and—"

Kelvin's fist connected with Linden's jaw, and Linden didn't finish his sentence. On that night, Kelvin forgot his wallet and returned home to overhear his brother asking his wife to run away with him. Without thinking, he threw his fist at Linden's jaw then continued to attack him. Linden tasted his blood and tried to shield himself from his brother's blows but couldn't stop the assault. Horrified, Sandra threw her body between the brothers.

"Stop this," she screamed frantically. "Just stop this. Don't do this. Please don't do this. One of you might kill the other."

"What do you expect? My brother is trying to 'tief' my wife."

The two brothers glared at each other. Linden wiped the blood from his nose. "You don't deserve her. She's a good woman, and all you do is drink and party. I love Sandra."

Sandra frantically grabbed and held Kelvin with all

her strength as he lurched at Linden. "I'm goin' to kill you. I'm goin' to kill you if you don't leave now." Kelvin said.

Linden, genuinely fearful of the threat, quickly ran out the door. Kelvin never left his wife's side that night, truly worried that she'd run away with his brother. Over the next few days, they were like newlyweds as they rekindled their love with outings to the beach and nights of heated lovemaking. The rum left his body, and Sandra remembered the man she first loved. But, after a few weeks in her company, he missed the boisterous frivolity of the rum shop. As soon as he heard that Linden was on a plane to Toronto, Kelvin kissed his wife on her lips. "I'm just going down the road to Rawle's. I won't be long."

She didn't see him until the next morning when he drunkenly returned home. And he found his way back to Rawle's the following day and every day after that. Her canvases became her company again, and she spent her time painting beach scenes as she remembered her afternoons with Linden. As the years passed, her husband spent more time at Rawle's, and she was left with memories of happier times. Her paintings became darker, as she avoided using reds, oranges, and pinks.

On the day that Linden arrives in Antigua after his long absence, Kelvin tells Sandra, "Me nah pick him up from the airport. Let him find his way to the hotel. I still can't stomach him." Then he leaves for Rawle's.

After having a few drinks, he calls his wife from the rum shop. "I'll pick up Linden at the airport and take him to the hotel. He's my brother and we need to make peace."

Linden is totally shocked when he hears his brother's familiar voice calling him when he clears customs. They eye each other warily but don't embrace; they are polite as they walk to the car, and Linden quickly notices that Kelvin stinks of rum. They leave the airport, and Linden sees the brightly coloured houses that adorn the hillsides, a scene so different to the nondescript glass towers of Toronto. He tries to relax but can't.

Kelvin breaks the uncomfortable silence. "We need a drink before I take you to the hotel. And it's time that you and I are man enough to clear the air."

And that's how they end up at Rawle's. The rum shop is still dingy, and Linden tries not to twist his face with disdain. He gingerly takes a seat at a broken table while Kelvin smiles in amusement at his brother's awkwardness. Before they begin to speak, Kelvin's cellphone rings.

He looks at the phone number on the display. "It's Sandra. That woman can't leave me alone, always wanting something."

His brother asks, "Shouldn't you answer it? She must be wondering where you are. Something could have happened to Auntie Jeannie."

"Believe me. Nothing is the matter. When I left, Auntie was still breathing. It's Sandra keeping a tight rein on me. You know how women stop."

Linden doesn't feel comfortable. "Let's go and see

Auntie Jeannie and Sandra first. Then we can come back. I think that's better."

"I know you still love my wife after all these years," Kelvin calmly states as he looks him directly in the eye. Then his voice rises, he slams his hands on the table, and everyone in the rum shop turns to look at them. "You think I forget! How can a brother do that to his brother? It's a good thing that Sandra is such a good woman. She will stay with me through thick and thin."

"Kelvin, can't we put this behind us? That's an old-time story."

"No, it's not. I think you can't wait to see her again."

The phone rings again. Kelvin sees it's Sandra; again he ignores it. "I'll call her when I'm good and ready. First, you and I need to have some words."

Kelvin orders drinks. As they arrive, he quickly drinks his and orders another. He is now quite inebriated and notices that Linden hasn't touched his glass. "What happened? You get soft living in Canada? Can't you have a drink with your brother?"

Linden takes a sip and the alcohol enters his system. His head spins.

Kelvin chuckles. "Now I know you get soft. It's cause you living in that cold place you forget how to drink."

The phone rings again; Kelvin lets out a big chupps. "This woman loves to nag me when me a drink me rum. You'd think that after all these years she know to leave me alone, nuh."

"Don't you think it could be important?"

"It someting stupid like the toilet block up."

"Then let me answer. If it was my wife, I'd answer."

Linden tries to grab the phone from Kelvin, but, even though he is drunk, Kelvin has his wits about him and grabs his brother's arm. "Nah answer my phone. Let me tell you dis: you can only speak to my wife when me say so."

"Look, I'm sorry for what I said and did years ago," Linden stutters uncomfortably. "Can't you leave it at that? You and Sandra are still together. Let it go, Kelvin. Let it go. I'm not here to mash up your marriage. I'm here to see Auntie Jeannie."

The brothers look at each other; they know they need to make a truce. Kelvin looks at him warily. "Dat better be de only reason that you come. Touch me wife and me go kill you. Sandra is a good woman. You know, when Auntie take in, Sandra tell her come live with us and she look after her like she her own mother. A man can't ask for a better wife."

Just as Kelvin speaks his last word, Linden hears her voice. He closes his eyes, desperately hoping that Kelvin doesn't notice his excitement.

"Why aren't you answering the phone, Kelvin?" Sandra yells. "I'm so tired of you and all of this!"

Linden opens his eyes. Sandra is still as beautiful and majestic as he remembers, and he quietly sighs with deep longing. But Sandra and Kelvin are so caught up in their argument that they don't notice him.

"I knew you'd be here 'cause this is where you always

are," she says with disgust. "Why didn't you answer the phone? You know your aunt is sick. Why, why, why do you choose to do these things? Auntie Jeannie just had a heart attack. She's in the hospital. They don't know how long she's going to last."

Kelvin looks stunned. "Are you serious?"

"You heard me. Auntie Jeannie is in the hospital. We'd better go before she dead."

The three of them hurriedly make their way to the hospital, and once Auntie Jeannie sees Linden, she smiles and takes her last breath. Kelvin looks at his dead aunt and tells his wife, "I need some fresh air."

He leaves and returns to Rawle's, where he takes a seat on his favourite corner stool. The bartender pours him a drink. Then he refills it, and Kelvin motions for him to put the bottle in front of him. Kelvin forgets about going home. And he misses his aunt's funeral.

Dogs sit outside the shop; flies cling to their mangy coats and buzz around their noses. The dogs lie at the bottom of the steps, either too lazy or too malnourished to be bothered by the flies. Sandra is sitting in her car looking at Rawle's and remembering all the events of the past week. She hates that she has to go inside and drag Kelvin from this decrepit place. She quickly tallies the years she's spent with him and the number of times she's saved him from killing himself with a bottle of rum.

When she enters the rum shop, the men stop banging

dominoes on the worn tables. The loud voices that are arguing politics and calypso music are hushed as the men look at her. They all know she's Kelvin's wife, and over the years, they've seen her come and fetch him many times. They say nothing but turn their heads towards Kelvin, and she follows their eyes to her husband. He's still sitting at the back of the room on an old stool. It looks hard; the wood is rotten and there is no cushion. She wonders how Kelvin can make such an uncomfortable place his home. A bottle of rum sits in front of him. His head lies heavily on the bar, and she isn't sure if he's asleep or passed out.

On his face there is a scraggly beard. His body appears to be covered with a film of dirt, causing him to look like a beggar; his body odour is foul and stale from a week of not bathing. When he hears the dominoes and chatter stop, Kelvin looks up for a moment with a dazed expression, thinking it is some man's woman or child making a scene about his absence at home. He sees Sandra, and he gives her a lopsided smile.

"You miss ya maannn, Sandrraaaa?" he asks. She grimaces as she smells the week of alcohol on his breath. "Mmmeee always knnooow youuu gooo commmme for mmmme."

"Kelvin, shut up."

"Sandraaaa, if you're not niccce, me nah commmme hoooommme with you."

She shakes her head in disbelief. "Are you planning to kill yourself in a bottle of rum this time?"

Sandra instinctively grabs the bottle of rum that sits in front of Kelvin. Despite his intoxicated state, he's quick and also grabs it. They both hold the bottle and tug and pull at it like it's a piece of gold. Neither of them is certain whose grip lightens, if it's Kelvin's or Sandra's, but when it does, the bottle falls to the ground and breaks. The liquid seeps through the cracks in the wooden floor and melts into the earth. The strong smell of alcohol permeates the room. They stare at the broken shards for a long time.

"Lllloook aat what you diiiiiid," Kelvin says.

"Kelvin, I don't have time for this crap. Do you see what you're doing to yourself? I'm so tired of this. I'm leaving." Sandra walks away.

He speaks in a whisper that's so low that Sandra barely hears him. "Ssssannndraa, nnnnnnaaahhh lllleave me here. Mmmeee go die without you."

She stops walking and turns around. He doesn't look away. His eyes tell her the words she heard from his lips. She remembers the man that she knows he can be. This weakens her resolve and she takes his hand. She pulls him from the hard stool. Her feet are heavy as she walks to the car. His hands feel cold in hers. He hangs his head low; they don't speak.

She drives quickly to their house, afraid that if she slows down she'll change her mind. Although she is tall and strong, it takes all of her energy to pull him into the house. He stumbles on a large object as they walk through the door.

"What'sss daaat?" he asks.

"It's nothing. I just moved some furniture," she hurriedly replies.

"Mmmmoveeee it. Sssommmeone gooo get hhhhurt."

"As soon as I have you settled in, I'll move it."

She takes a comb and tugs at the knots until his hair untangles. The razor slides smoothly along the grooves on his face; the week-old stubble falls to the ground. He looks blankly at her as she sweeps it away. Her husband is now an infant, and she helps him undress and then bathes him; layers of dirt wash down the drain. She takes the towel from the rack and dries his wet body.

He's afraid to look her in the eye and stands next to her with his head bowed, like a forlorn, repentant child. She takes his hand and leads him to their bedroom. He slumps onto the bed and pulls her down with him. He quickly falls into a deep slumber.

The air in the house is changed. It feels darker, and, even though the curtains are drawn open, the sun doesn't shine in the room. Kelvin sleeps. His drunken snores tells the house that he's home.

Kelvin holds her as he sleeps. His hands lie on her stomach, reminding her that he's still her husband. Once she craved that touch, but now his hands feel like a heavy object pinning her down. She is uncomfortable with this closeness as she remembers they haven't been intimate in a very long time because his rum habits took precedence over her.

While he sleeps, she gets up and makes a call. She quietly whispers on the phone so he doesn't hear her.

Then she hears Kelvin calling her name and she quickly puts down the receiver.

"Sandra," he yells from the other room. "Where are you, my wife? Where are you?"

She stands at the doorway; he's lying prostrate on the bed. The sun is high in the sky. It should have filled the room but doesn't. She stares out the window. A cloud hovers. Sandra remembers that she's never seen a cloudless sky. Kelvin awaits her response.

"I was just inside fixing something," she quietly tells him. She hopes he doesn't realize that she's lying.

"You are a good woman. I am blessed to have you."

She looks away. But he wants a response, and when he doesn't get one, he stumbles out of the bed. He moves closer to her and pulls her to him. She remains immobile as he presses his body into hers. He kisses her lips and keeps kissing them, but her mouth doesn't ease into his. She's only aware of the taste of the rum he's ingested for the past week. His hands touch the curves of her body. She stops him. "Get better first. You're in no state for this."

He nods and returns to bed, where he easily surrenders to its comfort. She hears him snoring. Then she leaves him and picks up the object that he'd stumbled on when he came through the door.

She quietly makes her way through the house with it and remembers that while Kelvin sat on the old, hard stool drinking rum, she went with Linden to the seashore. On that day, with the warm sun on their skin, he asked her if she still loved her husband. And she slowly shook her head because she was afraid to mouth the words.

"Marry me," he asked. "I know that we can be happy together because I want to make you paint beautiful canvases. Let's restart our clock."

With the suitcase in tow, she recalls that she looked at him and told him a secret. Two days before Auntie Jeannie died, a serious-looking man with a suit and briefcase visited her. Behind closed doors, they whispered, and a frail Auntie Jeannie called to her after the man left.

"Sandra." Her voice was weak and low. "When I became sick, you took me in and looked after me like I was your own blood. I never had children, but you are like my own flesh and blood. Now, I'm going to be a mother to you 'cause you need one bad, bad, bad. That man who just left this house is my lawyer. I've left my house with its pretty yard filled with yellow bells to you. And no one else. Nothing goes to your good-for-nothing husband."

Auntie Jeannie saw Sandra's eyes well with gratitude. She gently touched Sandra's hand with her weathered, frail ones. "I can't keep my tongue still anymore. My child, man who love rum, only love rum. He nah go change. Leave my wutless nephew and make a life for yourself."

Sandra looked at the sea, then she looked directly at Linden. "Auntie Jeannie gave me more than I ever dreamed or expected. I can paint colours again." Then she rested her head on his shoulder.

Linden was quiet for a long time before he spoke. "I guess you won't take up my offer to run away with me."

"I can't leave my husband for his brother," she slowly

responded. "But I still want you in my life. And right now I need your help to move."

"Only if you promise to visit me in Toronto," he added.

She smiled and nodded. They sat at the waterside with her head comfortably nestled on his shoulder.

Sandra is now standing at the door. Kelvin's snores are in the background. She takes a final look at the house she's shared with him. Her canvases are no longer on the walls. Linden helped her take them down and hang them at the quaint green house with yellow bells. Her suitcase easily slides out of the doorway. There is no loud thump as she closes the door.

Caught in a Chasm

"Are you alone, Tara?" Ken asked.

I nodded.

"It's been awhile," he said as he sat next to me.

We looked at each other in an uncomfortable silence in the café we once frequented. I didn't understand why he was here, nor did I ask that simple question.

To ease the strain, Ken called over the owner, Sherry. She knew us when we held hands; then she got to know me really well after Ken left and I came alone. On that first day, several months ago, I had ventured on my own into her establishment wearing a rumpled dress. As I am a tidy person, Sherry instinctively knew that Ken and I had had a bad tiff. She came over to me and laid her hands on my shoulder. "It'll be okay, Tara. One day the tears will be gone."

I didn't say anything and just stared blankly at her. Those were the first words I'd heard in a while because after Ken's abrupt departure, I locked myself away. Once he was gone, I began doing things I'd never done. I paced the floor till daylight. I cried for hours over melancholy love songs. I stared vacantly at the walls. During that period it felt like someone hit me over the head with a bat at regular intervals. Sleep eluded me and this played tricks on my mind.

That was why one night, at an hour when the moon snoozed because no one was awed by its glow, I looked outside. For some time I thought of venturing into the dark streets but was fearful that shadows would overwhelm me. I brushed aside my trepidations and finally stepped into the night. Darkness cloaked the world as I drifted along alleyways where scantily clad women were accompanied by large men. I followed them along dimly lit lanes, through a dark doorway and into a room that was abuzz with people and sounds. Here paint peeled from the walls, people danced hypnotically to sounds I'd never heard, dim lights obscured faces, and large sofas sat on the periphery to allow bodies to find compatible ones.

I found a corner and shocked myself as I began grooving to the beat of this room. For the first time in weeks, I closed my eyes and my heartache disappeared. I reopened them to find a man standing in front of me. We were the same height. Our hair was the same texture and colour. Our skin was tanned to the exact hue; our faces were the identical shape. If he were a girl, he'd be me, and if I were a boy, I'd be him. He wore a forest green shirt that he left unbuttoned, revealing a muscular chest. We played coy as we assessed each other. There was something so tantalizing about this stranger. I surprised myself because I felt a need to know more about him: his likes, his dislikes, his voice, his lips, his body. I smiled, giving him my consent, and he moved towards me. We touched, and like ice in a glass, my body melted. He whispered he was Jonathan, but I didn't reply; I just wanted to breathe him into me.

He spoke some words, but I don't remember them. I was only aware of the strong physical pull. That was why I guided him to a couch where we could lay together. I stretched my body against his and felt his arms wrap around me.

The sound of shattered glass surprised me, and I opened my eyes to realize that I was lying on a sofa with an unknown man in a room full of strangers. Before Jonathan realized what happened, I rushed out of the crowded room into the street. I ran for a long time and then stopped in front of a store. I looked at myself in the window. My hair was dishevelled, and my blouse was unbuttoned. I didn't fix them. I continued to wander the streets.

I arrived home as the sun sat at the brink of the horizon. I couldn't sleep. I daydreamed of Jonathan. We were alone on the dance floor. Slowly, he undressed me, and I stepped away from my clothing. We danced. Me naked, he half-clothed, our bodies touched, his skin, smooth and silky, softly caressed mine. Before the dance ended, he whispered, "I have to go." He slipped out of my arms and into the darkness. I stood there, naked and alone.

After that incident, my days became a void as my nights were filled with images of Jonathan. I wanted to see him. I took to drifting the streets, thinking about returning to the place where we met, but I couldn't find the courage to go through the door again.

It was the sound of Ken's voice that interrupted my thoughts. "Where are you, Tara?" he said. "You look like you're a million miles away. Did you hear me?"

Ken's question brought me abruptly back to the present. He was staring intently at me, waiting for a response. I wondered if he saw through my facade as I mumbled incoherent words. I wanted to flee to an island where I could sit on a deserted beach. My friends would be the animals whose homes were in those waters; my food would be the sweet fruit that grew on that lonely land. I didn't want Ken to know my heart anymore. I didn't want to answer his questions. Ken's deceit still felt like a blade was lodged in my body and blood was slowly oozing from the deep gash.

Amid all those thoughts, my eyes locked with Ken's. We were both silent. It was as if our minds drifted back to a time when we were in unison; our laughter rang in the air, our chatter was non-stop, our passion surged. I didn't want to find myself absorbed in the past, so I turned away. To my surprise, the sun was beginning to set. I looked around and saw the lunch customers were gone, and Sherry was setting the tables with candles and flowers for dinner.

I wondered where the time went and if I'd spent the entire afternoon sitting with Ken. I couldn't remember our conversation. I realized that my mind drifted while we sat, but I didn't know when this journey began. I worried that I revealed too much. In my confused state, I walked away, leaving Ken to sit alone. My eyes filled with tears as I left him. I walked to a park and sat on a bench next to a fountain that spouts water high into the air.

There was so much hurt inside. I knew that I didn't want to be alone again after experiencing love. I didn't want to get used to sleeping by myself on my lonely bed. I felt like I was the sole survivor of a nuclear holocaust, all alone with no one to love, no one to care for, and no one to talk to. I cried. People stared at me. I just kept on crying. I thought the sounds from the fountain would muffle my sobs, but they did not. My sobs grew louder and louder.

After seeing Ken, I couldn't think about anything other than him that night. I felt the walls closing in on me, and I needed to escape. That night I drifted; again I ventured onto dimly lit streets, walking through dark alleys, and past men who accosted me. I was drawn to the place where the music vibrated. That night I found the courage to re-enter the doorway. Once inside, I was transported from the dingy room to a world of infinite space. In this trance there were no walls. Here the people merged into one: the music, our rhythm, our bodies, the expression.

My eyes were closed absorbing the world I created. I opened them to see an image of myself. My heart raced hoping it was Jonathan. I pushed through the crowd, but he was not to be found. He disappeared like daylight moving quickly into darkness.

I leave and go home, where I stayed awake and stared into the black sky. His face appeared before me. I fantasized. He was an artist, perhaps a designer. His hands created masterpieces. The critics applauded his genius. He would dress me in gowns to show the world he cared. I knew I could love him, for his brown eyes told me of sorrow; his hands spoke of gentleness; his lips were passion. My daydream shifted. I met him on the dance floor. His hands touched the flowing fabric of my dress; it silently slid from my body. This time as I stood before him in my nakedness, he smiled in appreciation.

Jonathan became my world; once again, he filled the void in my life. I didn't fear being home anymore. I stopped going to Sherry's café. At first I welcomed him because he made me forget my loneliness and grief for Ken, but I found myself caught in a chasm, unsure of reality, and wondering if Jonathan was real.

Ken called as I mulled over those thoughts. There was no contact since our accidental meeting, and, in my daze, I couldn't remember if we met a week or two weeks ago. His voice was like an anchor, holding me in place so that my mind wouldn't stray far. He wanted to see me, and I agreed to meet.

He was comforting that day. He felt my agony but didn't intrude. Instead he spun tales that made me laugh and eased my mind. I told him I'd forgotten how much fun we once shared. He reminded me that we used to be friends. I looked at him to see that his eyes were still brown, his hair was still black, and he still laughed when I told him a joke, even if it wasn't funny. Then I told him something I wouldn't have before.

"I once thought you were perfect. There were even moments when I thought I wasn't good enough for you. Times have changed and I don't think that way anymore."

"I was never perfect, Tara," he confessed. "But you

made me feel like I was, and that was scary."

We were silent. I knew he wanted to say more, but I didn't need to hear his confession. I also realized that there was a reason why he wanted to see me. But I didn't want to hear his words, so I told him that it was time to leave. He paid the bill, and we walked to our old home. We said little as we strolled. Once we strolled hand in hand; that was a long time ago.

That night, I imagined the walls whispered to me. I didn't listen because I wanted to venture out. I wandered down those same dark alleys to the place where I met Jonathan. Finally, he was there. His dance was one of courtship as he twirled and dipped. I said nothing as I moved closer to him. I grabbed his hand and led him away. In the shadows, I thought I saw pain in his eyes. I understood, for I had my own sorrow.

I took him to my bed. He was, as I imagined, soothing like the stream as it flows through the valley. It was under the glow of candlelight when our bodies, glazed with sweat, took a break. During this interlude, I told him that where I came from the stars frolic in the skies at night, and the moon is a beacon that casts brilliant shadows on the land. There, the fish dance in the water, and the people dance on the land. I revealed to him that once I loved a man so deeply I forgot myself. This man broke my heart and left me alone to bleed. I said that I wanted to love again one day, but next time I'd remember me. Then I closed my eyes. I slept.

I woke to an empty bed. I touched my lips, and they

felt bruised from my night with Jonathan. I wrapped myself in the sheets. They smelled of his scents. I stayed in the bed where I laid with Jonathan and slept once more. I did not dream. A total blackness encompassed me, and I slept all day till night fell again. I awoke and sat in the darkness of the room, with only a lamp for company.

I once feared listening to the sounds of the house by myself. The tap would drip, the clock would tick, but until Ken left, I didn't notice them. Now, I need to learn how to sit in my home and hear the aching wood creak, the bolts shift into each other, the concrete settle.

Eventually, I left the bed and stood at the window. I stared out into the deep, dark sky. My mind was crowded with thoughts. I didn't look at the walls, nor did I venture into the streets. Finally, I listened to my congested mind.

Ken came into my bed when the sun was at its peak. We were totally satiated and fulfilled by nightfall, so the candles allowed our shadows to dance on the wall. I let him see my body in the daylight, my heart at midnight, and my soul in the moonlight.

Once upon a time Ken and I were astronauts who soared to the stars. Then we became earthlings who looked at the heavens and wondered if the celestial bodies exist. Knives leave wounds. Lovers carry weapons. On a hot, muggy day Ken plunged a blade deep into my heart. As the blood gushed, I wondered how this man, who once caressed my body and sucked my nipples, could make me bleed.

Daylight approached. I saw the moon fall into the

horizon in the west and the sunrise in the east, lighting up the sky with orange and pink flames. The newness of the day beckoned me to walk the streets. I smelled the freshness of the morning in the rising dew and listened to the melodic birds chirp. I searched the streets that led me to Jonathan. I walked for hours along roads where children played, adults shopped, and animals strolled, but none led me to a dark door and a mysterious man. My feet grew tired after hours of searching. Finally, I arrived at Sherry's café and sat in a seat that overlooked the street. As Sherry brought me a cup of coffee, I smiled brightly.

"It's been a while since you've smiled, Tara. It looks good on you," she said.

"It sure feels good," I replied in a light and buoyant tone. We didn't need to speak any further. She knew.

For the first time in months, I looked inquisitively at the people passing. I saw their figures, amongst them, a man of my height in a green shirt. He may have been Jonathan. My eyes followed his trail until all I saw was a dot of the clothing he wore, and, eventually, that faded.

Jumbies Don't Sleep

An earlier version of this story was published in *So the Nailhead Bend, So the Story End: An Anthology of Antiguan and Barbudan Writing* edited by Althea Prince

Tomorrow, I bury Mamma. Her head will be wrapped in a well-worn black scarf. And she will wear her favourite outfit, a beautiful lilac dress that she bought for my graduation, and she then donned it at my wedding and every other celebration she attended. Although we never spoke about her funeral, I know she'd want to be buried in this dress. It may sound strange, but I believe I'm hearing her say, "Just mek me look me best for dis last time."

Tonight, I'm in the house where we once lived, trying desperately to write her eulogy. The paper in front of me is blank: a crisp white sheet, forlorn and lost without letters, taunting me with its emptiness. I'm struggling to find words to pay homage to Mamma. This is so unlike me because as a journalist, writing is as easy and natural to me as the sea touching the shore. Why can't I find the words to say goodbye to the woman who raised me?

At times like this, Mamma would look at my furrowed brow and say, "Melanie, when you head have too many thoughts, it like one jumby dat haunt you. Sometimes, chile, you nah need to pressure yourself as much as you do. The answer always come when it want to come."

People always said that I inherited my serious side from Mamma. She was not known to smile, yet on those rare occasions when she did, her smooth, dark skin and dimpled cheeks came to life. While I called her "Mamma," on the island she was known as "Head-T." She began wearing a black head scarf when I was a small child, and I can still vividly remember the day she stopped showing the world her hair, even though more than twenty years have passed.

I was six years old when an incessant knock on the door and a voice woke me from my sleep. "Miss Evelyn, Miss Evelyn. Wake up, Miss Evelyn. Answer de door, Miss Evelyn, answer de door. Me need to talk with you."

Startled, Mamma and I both awoke at the same time, and, in my daze, I thought it was a dream. But as the voice kept calling for Mamma and there was constant knocking on the door, I knew this was real. I was a young child who found comfort sleeping in Mamma's bed, and, on that night, I felt it shift when she got up. Scared of being alone, I drowsily followed her into the living room, where she groggily opened the thumping door.

A man's words spilled into the house: "Miss Evelyn, you got to go to de hospital. Someting bad happen and tings—" The neighbour abruptly stopped speaking when he realized I was standing next to Mamma. He looked at her, his brown eyes conveying a message, and she instinctively read it.

In a shaky voice, Mamma firmly told me, "Go inside, Melanie. Me need to talk with dis man."

Obediently, I re-entered the house, where I peeped at Mamma through the window. As he spoke, I saw Mamma stagger and then fall. The neighbour grabbed her, his strong arm steadying and supporting her. He held onto her until she regained control. It was a distraught Mamma who ran into the house, tied her dishevelled hair with her black scarf, and told me, "Come, Melanie, we have to go to de hospital."

I put my small hand in her shaking one. Something was wrong, but I was helpless to do or say anything. The neighbour drove us to the hospital. The car was filled with silence. Mamma was quiet as she stared out the car window. Her eyes held a blank gaze and her lips quivered. This was so unlike her, and I knew something bad had happened.

My next memory is her wild sob when she saw my mother lying on the hospital bed with wounds, blood, and tubes. And then my voice joined Mamma's scream. At that moment, every other sound and thought was lost to me because my childlike voice cried, "No, no, not my mommy! Do something to make her better. This can't be, this can't be. Make my mommy better. She can't die. What will I do without her?"

Mamma pulled me to her, trying desperately to calm me, but I was a child losing her mother, and no one could offer me assurance. I was wild. I was frightened. But Mamma firmly hugged me as we sat next to my mother's hospital bed, where she lay motionless, comatose, lifeless. I knew my mother was dying, and it hurt. Mamma softly touched her tangled hair. "Bella, fight. Just keep fighting. Fight till you can't fight no more. Dis a tear me heart like nothing else. Me promise me go love Melanie and look after she no matter what. You me only chile, and me nah like how tings look. Dis not right atall, atall, atall."

Some people tell me that when someone is dying they look peaceful, but not my mother. Her face looked deeply pained. I always think it was because she was struggling so hard to live and didn't want to leave me. She never opened her eyes to see me one last time, but I believe she held on because she needed to know that I was in Mamma's care.

After the doctor told her that my mother was gone, Mamma screamed, and, in her deep agony, she pulled all of her glorious curly hair from her head, grabbing strand after strand until there was nothing left. Although her hair grew back, Mamma was never seen without a black head scarf. Once, when one of her church friends told her it was time to stop wearing the "head ties" because she'd grieved long enough, Mamma looked her in the eye. "Nah tell me wha fah do. You never bury your child, me de one who do dat. And nothing tall harder dan dat. Me wear dis head tie pon me head cause it hurt bad, bad, bad. And me go wear dis scarf till me dead cause it match me mood. How you expect me to wear someting bright when dat man who kill me only chile and she husband a walk de streets and not even spend a day in jail? Dat not right atall, atall, atall."

I lost both my mother and father and became an

orphan on a night when there was no moon. Though over twenty years have passed, I still remember the darkness of the night as we left the hospital and I held on desperately to Mamma for assurance.

A drunk driver killed my parents on Airport Road as they were making their way to my grandmother's home. While my father died instantly, my mother lingered long enough to see that I was in her mother's care before she joined her husband. The nurses told me she fought to live and it was a miracle she made it to the hospital. My mother never regained consciousness and didn't get the chance to look at me one last time or even say, "I want to see you grow up. This isn't right! Mothers don't die on their children." She never saw her mother's dimples again and couldn't tell her, "I don't want to leave my little girl. Please take good care of her."

Although both of my parent's bodies were a tangled mess, the man who caused the accident didn't have a scratch on his body. When the police arrived at the scene, they astutely noted his inebriated state as he drunkenly mumbled to them, "Call my father. He is a big man in the government."

With those words, the uniformed officers forgot they were to uphold the law as they secretly began contemplating the lucrative bribe they could pocket. They helped him to their police vehicle, where they gave him a bottle of water and told him to wait while they covered my father with a cloth. As the ambulance drove my unconscious mother to the hospital and my father's lifeless body lay on the ground with a grey blanket covering him, the man's father arrived. The important government official quietly noted the dead man and then learned from the police about my mother's critical state. He told the officers that this was a family matter as he handed them several crisp hundred dollar bills and promised them there would be more. The police escorted the drunken man to his father's car and conveniently forgot to charge the man who killed my parents.

I don't think this drunken man felt any remorse over their deaths because he never sent a wreath, and he was always at the rum shop with a drink in his hand. I grew to know his face, and even though years have passed, I can still vividly recall how he looked. He was a short, stout, nondescript brown man with a small neck and bloodshot eyes. If it weren't for the accident that gave him infamy, he'd be unmemorable to most people.

Every time my grandmother saw him driving his immaculate white car on the road, which seemed to happen on a regular basis, she'd cuss, "You kill me chile. And you kill she husband. You tek dem away from me and leave dem only chile here on dis earth. You one bad, bad, bad man."

As soon as he heard her voice, the man slouched into his seat to hide from her. Then he'd put his foot on the pedal of the car, hoping to escape her verbal tirade.

"God go judge you," she'd yell. "Me nah have to do one ting in dis life to mek you pay for dis wrong you cause. Me know de man upstairs go mek sure you find your place in hell."

People who were standing on the sidewalk would stop what they were doing as they watched the drama unfold. Because of my grandmother's tirades, everyone on the island knew what he'd done, and, oftentimes, someone joined my grandmother and also cussed the man. As a child, I was very embarrassed, but, as I grew older, I didn't care. My grandmother wasn't a crazy woman, but she was angry. When my parents died, I was six years old, while she was a spritely sixty-year-old with a meagre income who was now my sole caretaker. A deeply religious woman, she prayed morning and night: "God give me de strength to last till Melanie become a woman. Please nah tek me yet."

Mamma worried incessantly about my future. Life was good, and her prayers were always answered. There was the kindly businessman who paid for my schooling, and the people in the church who made sure my grandmother had enough food on the table. Mamma always said, "God always look out for us cause we believe."

My success in school led to a scholarship at a foreign university that took me away from the island and my grandmother. But Mamma made sure she found the money to attend my graduation ceremony, where she looked like the proudest parent in the world. After the service, she hugged me so hard that I couldn't breathe. And, with her eyes filled with tears, she proudly handed me a small gift box.

I shook my head. "Mamma, you didn't have to do this. I don't need anything. I'm just happy to have you here."

"Dis belong to you," she replied firmly. "Open it."

In the box sat a delicate gold chain that looked vaguely familiar, and I tried to recall where I'd seen it.

Smiling sadly, Mamma's hands quivered as she clasped the necklace around my neck. "For so long me did want to give dis to you, but me a wait for de right time, cause me didn't want you to lose it. Dis belong to you mother. How I wish she and you father could be here to see you!" She added, "Melanie, if the Lord take me now, me okay with dat, cause you grow into a fine woman."

I was very scared when I first came to live with my grandmother after my parents' death. My loss was a tragedy unlike anything Shakespeare wrote. I could have easily withdrawn from the world and become a hibiscus flower that stayed in its pod, but Mamma wouldn't let that happen. In those first days after my parents' death, she cradled me in her lap and reassured me that we'd be okay. "God don't punish the good," she said. "He just give us challenges to make sure we ready for heaven."

As a small child, one's imagination is wild; mine was filled with fears and dread after the accident. I couldn't sleep because my biggest nightmare was that my parent's jumby might haunt me. And when I confided this to Mamma, my ever-resourceful grandmother replied, "Melanie, me know fah sure dat your parents' jumby nah go hurt you. Dem did love you so."

She stared deeply into my brown eyes, which looked like her own and told me a poem:

Jumbies don't sleep,
But they weep
Cause they miss seeing you
So pretty when dressed in blue.

Jumbies don't sleep,
But at night they quietly creep
Into the bed where you lay,
Keeping you safe for another day.

Mamma and I recited those words night after night. With time, we added new verses that reflected our day; sometimes the words were serious, and at other times they were funny because our day was filled with mirth. But those words kept my parents alive for me. That poem saved me, and I believe it saved my grandmother. It was our way of keeping my parents in our lives and telling them about what we did. Not only did that poem give me comfort, but it also taught me the power of language. I told Mamma that she made me a writer because of those words, but she never believed me. She always said, "Dats who you were meant to be."

Alone in the room, I feel her memory cuddle me as I repeat the poem. The words slide easily and sweetly from my lips. As I speak, I feel Mamma standing next to me with her head tie and dimpled cheeks. I look at her with tears. "Is it okay? Can I do this? It's not traditional, but it's us." Mamma nods her approval, and then she is no longer in the room. The pen glides on the paper, the words flow, and I begin to write her eulogy, filling the white sheet with our special poem.

Secrets Never Shared

"Oh my God, I can't believe it's you, Dionne! You look absolutely amazing! Even better than I remember," Shayne gushed as he enthusiastically threw his arms around me. In his zeal, he didn't notice that I'd stepped away from his embrace. Oblivious, he continued, "How many years has it been? And what the heck are you doing here?"

I never expected to see Shayne again. Now, with him standing in front of me, a million thoughts and emotions bubbled to the surface—anger, disgust, fury. This wasn't a meeting I imagined or wanted. There we were, two old lovers, standing on a crowded sidewalk, quietly assessing each other. As I looked at this man, who I once loved blindly, my sole goal was to get away from him as quickly as possible.

"I moved here around a year after we broke up. This city is my home and has been for quite some time. I guess the better question to ask is what are you doing here?" As much as I tried to be cool, I knew he heard the edge in my voice.

He stepped back and looked at me, his cool grey eyes taking in everything but not revealing his emotions. In that moment, though neither of us spoke, we both quietly acknowledged why my words were like ice.

When he finally replied, his voice was composed and deep, the way I always remembered. "I moved here a couple of months ago. What a great city! I work over there." His hands pointed to the skyscraper across the street.

Instinctively, I mumbled something about working in the building next door. Then I began to squirm uncomfortably, biting my lip and shifting my body from side to side, thinking that I shouldn't have replied. A voice inside me wanted to scream because this wasn't supposed to happen; he was too close and could easily knock on my door. That's why I lied to get away from him. "I've got to go—I have a big deadline. It was great seeing you after all this time."

He shoved his business card in my hand. "Call me, Dionne. It'd mean the world to see you again."

I'm not sure if he read the insincerity behind my promise to call, and I didn't care if he saw me throw his card in the garbage as soon as I turned the corner. The truth was I never wanted to see him again.

The last time I saw Shayne was from my balcony ten years ago. On that early morning, as the sun began to rise and filter through the blinds, Shayne's brown skin glistened with day-old oils. Our voices were whispers of excitement as we solidified our plans to move in together now that we were graduating from university. The darkness of the room turned to shadows and then to light. I watched him in the dim light of my room. His grey eyes were unique, quietly blending into his smooth chocolate skin, giving him an air of exoticism.

No more than a minute after he left, I impulsively ran to my balcony. From my seventh floor apartment, I saw his athletic frame climbing into his car. I called to him. My sound carried in the wind, and he looked up. Even though he was a dot on the road, I saw him smile. Then he waved. I stood, rooted to the spot, wholly enraptured as I watched him drive away.

I never saw him again. My next memory was his voice, raspy and distant, telling me that he needed his space. And then he confided that he hadn't been honest with me because he was going to teach in Africa and thought it was best that we didn't see each other again. After he hung up, I stood alone holding the phone. He never called to say goodbye. I waited by the phone, expecting to hear it ring and hear his voice telling me he'd changed his mind.

Shayne and I met during our last year at undergrad. He was a political science major, and I studied journalism; his dreams were to change the world, while I wanted to write about his revolution. I fell deeply and blindly in love with him, ignoring the warnings from my friends that wanderlust was in his blood. He settled into me so easily and sweetly, better than a comfortable pair of sneakers.

I can barely remember those first few weeks after he left. My next recollection was returning home to live with my parents, who were shocked to see me because they thought I was starting a life with Shayne. I was their last child, born when they thought that it was impossible to conceive. By the time I was twenty, they were in their sixties. They were good, church-abiding people who tried to keep as much of this modern world out of their life, for they thought it was filled with bawdy images and callous people. I had a hard time explaining Shayne's disappearance; they couldn't understand why he'd walk away from me after making a promise. They believed that your deeds aligned with your words. Alone in that house, with my parents hovering around, I desperately wanted to speak with Shayne to let him know where I was and how I was, but I couldn't contact him. He left no forwarding address. As I reacquainted myself with my childhood bed, I realized that if I hadn't had so many reminders of Shayne, I'd wonder if he was real or if he was some person I'd seen on a movie screen.

A year later, I left my parent's home to restart my life. Amongst my belongings was an ornate jewellery box decorated with dazzling mother-of-pearl, where I stored pictures of Shayne's smiling face, photos of us at different events, poems he'd written for me, and stubs from movies we'd seen. Once it was filled with our memories, I locked it and threw the key into the garbage. That box came with me as I began my new life in a home far from everything and everyone I knew, where I displayed that ornate case on a ledge in the living room. For a while, it taunted me with memories, but I always fought the compulsion to open it. People came to my home, and they admired the box's beauty. Some were curious about its contents, but I always told them I bought it locked and didn't know what was inside.

With time, Shayne became a memory that was confined to this box. That was when I removed the case from the living room and put it in the back of a cupboard, where it gathered dust.

Shortly after that, I met Terence. For him, it was love at first sight. I thought our meeting was a nice coincidence, but he always says, "It was destiny."

I didn't think anything of it when I tapped on the shoulder of a well-dressed stranger because I was lost. "Excuse me, but can you help me? I need directions."

That's when a man with strong, broad shoulders turned around and stared at me for a long time before he replied, "Of course I can. I'm always happy to help a pretty lady." I was surprised by his warmth and thought it was odd when he escorted me to my destination. As we made our way along the crowded sidewalk, he introduced himself as Terence and asked, "Where are you from? Your accent is different, and I don't think you're from around here."

I replied that I'd recently moved. He then told me about all the wonders of the city, but before he finished, I'd reached my destination and rudely interrupted, "I hate to cut you off, but I've got to run. I'm late for my appointment."

An hour later, as I left the building, I heard someone say, "Well, you could have said thank you." I turned around and there was Terence. I shook my head and laughed. He smiled, and in that instant, I knew he was going to be someone special in my life. He asked, "Did you think you could get away from me so easily?" I knew the answer was no.

Ours was not a love to be stored in an old jewellery

box gathering dust in the back of a cupboard: it was so much more. It was the jewellery one wears every day because the gems glisten and the gold never tarnishes. I quickly discovered that Terence was not impulsive, but he was a romantic who believed in fate. and that's why he felt he couldn't let me go when we first met. Through him I learned about love between a man and a woman. That was why, on a sacred morning, we wed to the smiling eyes of our families and friends.

I went home to my husband and daughter, Dara, and tried to forget about Shayne. A week ago, I discovered that I was pregnant again. Terence and I were very excited about our new baby, and each morning as he awoke he'd shake me from sleep. I'd climb into his arms as he told me, in his husky voice, about the new name he dreamt for the life that was growing inside me.

Although this was not my first child, everything about this pregnancy felt different. When Dara was in my womb, other women shared their birth stories and told me each pregnancy is unique. Now I finally understood. I wondered how Dara would adjust to a new brother or sister. Whenever I looked at my beautiful daughter, I always acknowledged that her father left his stamp on her.

Terence was excited about our expanding family. He gave me love, respect, and trust. Our relationship was an eternal flame that would flicker but never burn out. Despite the strength of our bond, I kept my accidental meeting with Shayne to myself. He was locked inside a box, and I believed that this was a secret that should be kept closed; there wasn't a need to pry open that rusted lock.

I stepped out during my lunch break a few days later to hear Shayne's voice. "Do you mind if I join you?"

I turned around to see him smiling at me, his grey eyes twinkling. He was carrying a bouquet of flowers—irises. That was once his flower of choice. They were beautiful, but I didn't reach out to take them. I looked at him with suspicion. "Are you waiting for me?"

"I don't want you to think that I am stalking you, but, yes, I wanted to see you again, and I somehow thought you wouldn't call." The flowers were outstretched in his arms, but I didn't accept them.

"Would you blame me?" I asked.

"I don't think I should answer that question. But I'd really like to clear the air with you. Can we have lunch?"

I didn't want to say yes, but I didn't know how to say no. And that was how I found myself sitting with Shayne.

"I never thought we'd meet again," he confided. "And I can't tell you how glad I am that we did. I've always wondered what happened to you."

I didn't reply. What was I to say? I didn't want to share all the events of my life since he so selfishly disappeared. And I know my eyes hardened with those thoughts. He saw their impenetrable glaze and switched the subject. He spent five years in Africa before returning home. It was a promotion that brought him across the continent. As he spoke, his political convictions came back to life, and I was pulled into our youthful passion, fondly remembering our old love. And suddenly, he looked into my eyes, and I stared back into his own haunting ones. For a moment I felt myself weakening. I thought of secrets never told and words that were never spoken; it was like that box in the cupboard needed opening.

He broke the reverie with a long-awaited apology. "I'm sorry for how I behaved. It was a selfish act and one you didn't deserve. It has always bothered me. And I was too ashamed to contact you."

I listened to his words that were spoken too late, and, in the heat of the moment, I foolishly expressed those feelings. "Shayne, I wish I knew what was going on in your mind. Things would be so different today."

He moved his hands to touch me. He felt so strong. That was when he looked into my eyes and asked me a series of questions.

"Are you married?"

"Yes."

"How long?"

"Seven years."

"Do you love him?"

"That's a silly question."

"No, it isn't. And you didn't answer."

"Yes, I love him. And I'm not saying anything further about Terence."

"Is he as boring as his name?"

"That's my husband, so don't disrespect him."

"I apologize. Do you have any kids?"

"Yes, a daughter. We're expecting another one. I'm three months pregnant."

"You've been pretty busy. I never thought you'd want kids so young. I always pegged you as the career type—one day the editor of some large magazine. I remember your speaking about writing a book. Where did those dreams go?"

"Life takes us on a different course and you can't fight it. I'm very happy with the way things turned out."

"Are you? Whatever happened to all those dreams?"

"They didn't go away. Terence tells me they're on pause. I believe him."

"Dionne, I must confess, when I look at you and see how radiant you are, I often wonder if I made the biggest mistake of my life."

I looked directly at him, and the firmness behind my words shocked me. "I can assure you that you did."

He laughed, and it went to his eyes. It was a throaty laugh and shook my foundation. I realized how often I'd heard it. That was the moment when I recognized his impact on my life. I'd foolishly thought it was behind me. Did first love have to haunt you as much as he did? I panicked. I needed to stop his questions before he got any deeper, before he realized that he could wreck my life again, and before he made me break open a rusted lock. I told him I had to leave because there was a deadline at work. He knew I was lying and grabbed my hand. I felt his warmth, and again I looked into his eyes that seemed to cling to my soul. I was desperate to escape before he realized he still held some sway on my life.

"Can I see you again, Dionne?"

I didn't answer. The truth was I wasn't sure what he wanted, and I didn't want to find out. That's why I gave him the wrong phone number for my office and accepted the flowers he brought. I threw them in the wastebasket at the side of my desk, but they didn't wither. The cleaner forgot to pass by my desk for the entire week, and they sat there in the garbage, slowly dying.

That evening, I went to the cupboard and took the ornate box filled with Shayne's memories from its hidden nook. Years had passed since I'd touched it. It lay in my lap, a layer of dust taking away the shine from the mother-of-pearl. There was a strong urge to open it, and I would have given in to the desire if Dara hadn't called my name. I hurriedly pushed the box back inside the cupboard. Yet, I felt Shayne's eyes haunting me wherever I turned. My husband noticed my nervousness, and though he knew that the key to the box was lying in some long-forgotten garbage pile, I confided that Shayne now lived in our city. He became uneasy after I spoke.

"Do you still have feelings for this man?" he asked.

"You know I don't. Anyway, I don't want to talk about this."

Terence trusted me. He was a stoic who understood my moods and never argued with me when I wouldn't communicate. Most importantly, Terence was confident in our bond. Although he knew there was part of me that he couldn't penetrate, he'd didn't try. And being the man he was, he left me alone after our brief discussion. He accepted my past was part of the old jewellery box that was gathering dust in the back of our cupboard. He knew that I had thrown away the key before he entered my life. And he believed that I didn't want to pry the box open.

The next time I saw Shayne was on a Saturday afternoon. Terence, Dara, and I were driving home on the highway. Just in front of us, a car hit another, and the highway was at a standstill. Dara, bored, was sitting in the backseat and, despite my disapproval, kept rolling down the window and calling to the people in the nearby cars. She was a mischievous child, and, from the front seat, I could see her eyes twinkle as she yelled out the window.

As the traffic wasn't moving, I looked around. I peered at the car next to me, immediately recognizing the profile of the man. My body stiffened as my breath came in hurried gasps; my feet felt heavy, like they were cemented to the floor. I wished that I was somewhere else and prayed that the traffic would move.

My husband heard my gasp and looked at me. He saw me staring into the car at Shayne. Although Terence only knew Shayne from a photo, he knew it was him. We both looked at each other, and for a moment it was like we were strangers. He wasn't sure what I was going to do. And I was too nervous to say anything.

Shayne was looking in front of him, his gaze bored and impatient. But, then he heard Dara calling to people and followed her voice. He turned his head and immediately recognized me. There was a look of pure joy in his eyes, and he quickly read the panic on my face. He was puzzled by my reaction and peered deeper into my car, where he met Terence's stony gaze. He inspected Terence for a second, and then he looked into the backseat, his eyes resting on Dara. He couldn't stop looking at my daughter. The tick of my watch echoed loudly in my ears.

In her mischievousness, Dara turned down the window and called to Shayne, her grey eyes catching Shayne's and revealing my secret. They stared at each other: one out of curiosity, the other out of shock. Through the glass, Shayne looked at me with the same grey eyes his daughter inherited. His shock turned to pain, and it transcended my fears. His loss was heavier than the secret I was forced to carry.

In that second, we both faced the gravity of our decisions so many years ago. I felt his gaze penetrating me. There was a part of me that wanted to free myself and step back in time, but I couldn't. I thought he would roll down his window or open the car door and try to change our lives, but then the traffic began to move. The car behind him honked its horn, and he continued to look at me through his grey eyes. I turned away. I didn't want to read what they said. The horn behind him grew louder, and he was forced to flow with the traffic.

Tamarind Stew

An earlier version of this story was published in *The Bluelight Corner: Black Women Writing on Passion, Sex, and Romantic Love* edited by Rosemarie Robotham

Before I met Tony, I wrote stories. He wanted to hear them but couldn't find the time. There were so many things I wanted to tell Tony but never did. So he didn't know that I began to write when I was eight, or that when I first learned to read, I found the pictures in the books more exciting than the words because the plots all sounded the same. There was always a princess being saved by a prince.

Tony was the first man I kissed. As I grew into womanhood, I watched him grow from a gangly teen into a tall brown man with smooth skin and strong bones. His eyes were alert and captured everyone around him, but they shone when he was with me. There was a time when it seemed that Tony couldn't do without me. When the sun rose, he'd make his way in the half light to my house and lightly throw pebbles at my bedroom window. I'd sneak past my mother's room in my short see-through nightgown to be with him. In the early morning, his lips held the freshness of the dew.

Many mornings, as we sat at the seashore, we would imagine what lay beyond the sea. Our home was an island ten miles wide and ten miles long. When I sat at the shore with Tony's body pressed into mine, the horizon seemed endless.

It was a hot afternoon when Tony and I first made tamarind stew. The sun was directly above when Tony arrived with a bag of tamarinds in his hand. Before we met, I'd pick tamarinds off the tree and eat them. Tamarinds have an overpowering sourness that is peppered by a faint sweetness, and I enjoyed bombarding my senses with their distinctive taste. Tony loved tamarind stew because he could disguise the sourness with brown sugar. I had never made tamarind stew until that hot afternoon when Tony taught me.

The first time we shelled tamarinds and poured them into a pot of boiling water, we nearly burned down the house. As the pot simmered on the stove, Tony's hands led me to the bedroom. The tamarinds melted in the water. They came together and bubbled till the cover of the pot clinked from the steam, and soon the pot was on fire.

The burnt pot did not stop our desire, and a few days later we attempted to make tamarind stew again. While the pot simmered on the stove, I sat on the kitchen counter. Tony stood in front of me. With my arms wrapped around his shoulders, we both peered into the pot and saw the tamarinds dissolve and thicken. After he poured brown sugar into the stew, his lips tasted of steam. When it cooled, Tony dipped his hand into the pot, and I licked the stew from his fingers. While we ate, a soft breeze blew through the window and caressed our skin.

I never heard fairy tales until I was six. My mother couldn't read, but she bought me book filled with beautiful pictures of powerful lions and colourful birds. There were large castles with princes and princesses. As I studied the enchanted animals and fairy-tale people, I created stories. I imagined their world and the lives they led. But my stories never had endings because I didn't know how to finish them. I just kept inventing new ways to live.

My first grade teacher was the first person to read me a fairy tale. Her voice droned the story in a flat monotone. As she turned the pages of the book I had treasured, the animals lost their magic. The castles were now hovels, and the people were no longer immortal. From the sound of her voice, I knew my toys did not come to life at night.

When my period didn't come, Tony smiled and said it was late. I wasn't sure. I drank some awful-tasting teas that tore my insides apart. Tony didn't know. When the blood flowed, I told him he was right. He believed me because we made tamarind stew. He didn't know how my body ached when I stood over the boiling pot. I didn't want to be a mother. The stories I invented didn't have children. The world I lived in had too many. The women dedicated their lives to them. They were worn and tired by the end of the day and often forgot to tell their children that the stories they read at bedtime were not real.

My mother didn't read me stories at bedtime. She didn't know about enchanted castles and handsome princes until I told her.

When I was eight, I read her a fairy tale.

She said, "That's not real life."

Then she told me the only story she knew. People were once chained and led across the ocean. They worked until they died. They were buried in unmarked graves. I told her that was a horrible story. She said it wasn't a story.

In the first tale I wrote, dragons conquered the world. Goliath survived in this story. When I read it in class, my teacher shook her head in disbelief. She told me it was blasphemous. I didn't understand what she meant. I thought it was a compliment because my story was different. All the other girls' stories had the same plot. It went like this: "I went to the market with my mother to buy fish. The prince was passing by in a carriage. When he saw me, he thought I was the most beautiful woman in the land. He stopped his carriage and told me to hop in. As we rode around the land, we fell in love."

Tony and I graduated from school at the same time. Though I was the more adept student, he got the better job. We worked different hours and saw less of each other. He said he was busy, but he was often just liming with his friends. I spent my time with my stories. Tony believed I was daydreaming. I wanted Tony to listen my stories, but he always had an excuse. Eventually, we fought.

After my outburst, I walked to the shore and stared at the horizon. The sea lapped gently at my feet. It was warm and told me nothing. A ship sat on the horizon. It did not move. I walked back to St. John's with no answers. The roads were narrow. People looked at me as I made my solitary way along the streets. My mother's image followed me as I walked. I thought of her life and I wasn't sure if I could walk alone as she had. That was why I never again asked Tony to listen to my stories.

One afternoon, when the breeze was still and the sweat dripped from our bodies and sticky tamarind stew simmered on the stove, Tony proposed. I cried. He saw the tears and told me he wished I had smiled instead. I didn't know why I cried. Nor did I understand why I accepted. The love that Tony and I shared was fading.

After the proposal, I asked my mother, "What do you think of Tony?"

She said, "He won't hit you."

"But he's no prince."

"Julie, there are no princes."

"But Tony doesn't know my soul or listen to me when I cry."

"No man ever heard me, Julie."

On the day of the wedding, large clouds covered the sun and allowed me to sleep. In my dream, a prince stood at the balcony of a castle. The people stood below him. His face was waxen as he waved to the crowd, which responded adoringly. I stood apart from the people. I felt that if the prince saw me, he would fall in love with me. My attire was shabby, and I believed that this was why he did not notice me. I rushed home and put on another gown more elaborate than the one I had been wearing. I returned to the castle, but still he did not see me. Once more, I journeyed to my house and changed my clothes, to no avail. I kept changing my ensemble, but he never wavered from his mechanical role of waving to the masses. Finally, I put on a wedding gown, sure that this would get his attention. On my way back to the castle, I fell into a hole filled with water. Startled, I woke up. To my surprise, my bed was soaked and my body was drenched in water. My mother stood next to the bed with an empty bucket.

"It's a chore, Julie."

I got up, wet and dazed from my sleep.

"What?" I replied.

"Love."

The sun did not shine that day; strange clouds hovered above. I was unsure of the hour. A spell left me numbed. My mother told me it was nerves.

Tony stood tall and strong as I walked down the aisle. His stance was majestic, and his smile told me he believed I was a princess. His eyes glittered like the diamond upon my finger. At the reception, the guests congratulated us as the sun became a large red ball in the sky and started its descent beyond the horizon. In the semi-darkness, I recalled all the fairy tales that I'd read. I stared at the orange sky with Tony at my side; his familiar body was pressed against mine. Nothing felt new even though everything I wore had never been worn before. I remembered how, earlier that day, I stood at the altar and sworn everlasting love to Tony. Even that vow was not new. Tony had heard me whisper those words many nights, but this was my first public declaration. Everyone in the room believed our story had begun. I alone knew it had ended.

Now I am married, and Tony is never home. He tells me he is working, but I hear his voice at the rum shop. He never asks what I write. He does not concern himself with my needs. His wish is always the same: tamarind stew. One morning, as the cock crows, I realize that Tony has grown into a man who will never again throw pebbles on my window, so I decide to forget that sound.

My stories have no audience. I am tired of the echo that carries on the wind. I dream about the people who will respond to my words. The man who lies with me at night does not know this. His familiar face will not be in the audience that applauds my work.

I think about all the things I've never told Tony. He has never heard me say, "My mother couldn't read and so she couldn't dream." He does not know that when I write, I touch my empty womb. I wonder if I'll read stories to my unborn children in the dull monotone of my first grade teacher.

I learned to read, so I know I'll be a different woman than my mother. She taught me to dismiss fairy tales, but she sent me to school to master reading them. She unleashed my imagination but didn't tell me what to do with it. I have lived my whole life with each foot in an unmatched shoe, and I've walked with uneven footsteps. Now I shall discard those mismatched shoes, and I will read my stories out loud.

It is late, well after midnight, and the moon is obscured by the clouds the night Tony hears my story. I have spent months writing this story, and I want Tony to be the first person to hear it. The dampness in the air tells me that rain is on its way. Before it can fall, I do something I have never done: I go to the rum shop where Tony limes with his friends, and I stand outside and call him. Because he is in a drunken stupor, he comes to me. I tell him to listen, and he does. I read him the story of an unknown god who defies the one named Tony. This god allows servants to become masters and love to defy tradition. I do not describe this god, nor do I give it a gender. It is nameless, faceless.

When I finish, Tony shrugs and says, "Nice. Now I know what you do with your spare time."

He walks back into the rum shop. He lifts a glass to his lips. I hear his voice chattering amongst his friends. He does not discuss my story.

The rain falls. It begins in little drops that become larger and larger. I walk in the downpour. It is hot and refreshing on my skin. The darkness of the night does not frighten me. As I walk, I shield the papers of my story from the water. My clothes cling to my body, and my hair looks like a mop. I take off my shoes and sink my feet into the mud that rolls freely down the road. When I get home, I climb into the bed that Tony and I share. My muddied body leaves dirt marks on the sheets and on the mattress. The rain sounds like a steel band playing music in the yard. I fall asleep writing words to the melody.

Feel-Good Thing

As zany as our feel-good thing is, it isn't something my friends and I planned. While some women get together to laugh while indulging in a decadent slice of chocolate cake or spend time basking in their sorrows over a bottle of wine, my friends and I are different. Yes, there is food and there are drinks, but we are playful and giddy because we indulge in the girlish game of dress-up.

My trio consists of me and my two best friends, Mena and Shari. I am considered the quietest of the group, but that doesn't mean that I am not without a quirky streak. Mena always says that I surprise people because they initially think I'm a wallflower until I'm afire; she likens me to a pot that simmers on the stove for a long time before it comes to a sudden violent boil.

As we are an unconventional set, it is inevitable that we'd find a unique way to deal with life's hurdles. Our feel-good thing came into existence on a hot, hazy summer's day before the heat began to clog the air.

Mena, Shari, and I languidly strolled the Danforth, briefly glancing at the busy restaurants and, every now and then, getting a flavourful whiff of the scrumptious Greek food. We were searching for that perfect place to sit, eat, and talk. With our penchant for gaiety, we liked places that didn't tell us to be quiet. As close friends, we often got together to laugh, but there were times when we needed each other for solace from one of life's many assaults. On that day when our dress-up game began, my life felt like a shattered glass lying on the floor; I was still looking for the dustpan to sweep it up.

Earlier that day, I'd called Mena to unload my problems; there is nothing like a Mena talk. She's very direct after years of listening to people's problems in her career as a psychotherapist. Her words are without adjectives, embellishment, or exaggeration, like a computer that clearly dissects a problem and tells the answer. If you'd never met her and just spoke with her, you'd be shocked to discover that she has long, wavy hair and a bodacious walk that turns heads. On first impression, men think she is an airhead and treat her like she can only count from one to ten; however, once she begins talking, they quickly realize that she can calculate the most complex calculus formulas. She once told me, "There is nothing called a dumb woman, but there sure are a number of men who do stupid things in their relationships." Although she spends her days listening to an inordinate amount of people, her clients' problems haven't affected her; she's happily married with two wonderful teenagers.

As I confided to her, she interrupted me. "Stop talking. It's time for the girls to get together. This is when you need your women friends."

Shortly after that, the three of us were walking on the Danforth. Mena and I were caught up with our discussion.

"Hey, Shari, you've been silent. What do you think?" I turned to ask her. "You know I love to hear what's going on in your mind."

To my surprise, Shari wasn't with us. Mena and I stopped walking and looked around. Because of my imposing height, I easily gazed over the heads of the pedestrians walking on the busy sidewalk and spotted Shari's spiky orange hair in the distance. I yelled at her, but she was too far away to hear me above the din of the traffic. Mena and I quickly retraced our steps. Finally, we were next to her, but she didn't seem to notice us. She was standing in front of a store window and was so deeply mesmerized by the display that she didn't take in anything around her.

Initially, I thought Shari didn't hear us because she was obsessing over some "must have" fashion item in the window and was convincing herself this was another article of clothing she couldn't live without. But I quickly realized the display wasn't what I'd expected, and I, too, was transfixed.

This wasn't a window display; it was a story. The scene seemed so real that I forgot the mannequin was an inanimate plastic object; here was a woman standing in front of a large mirror in a flowing white gown made from an iridescent, silky material, beautifully contoured to her slim waist and adorned with sparkling crystals. She smiled secretly as she admired herself in a dazzling tiara and glimmering silver shoes. She was the embodiment of a bride who was checking her image, making sure everything was perfect before she walked down the aisle to meet the man of her dreams.

"Isn't she beautiful?" Shari gushed.

"She looks real," I replied.

Shari continued, "I know it sounds crazy and totally bizarre, but I've always wondered what it'd be like to wear one of these decadent, beautiful gowns."

Mena impulsively grabbed Shari's hand. "Here, put this on."

Without thinking, Shari slipped on Mena's engagement ring, and before I realized what was going on, Mena led us into the bridal fantasyland. All around were young women, glowing with love, sporting perfectly sculpted, youthful bodies and donning gowns that'd make Cinderella envious. They posed in front of friends and family, who "oohed" and "aahed" over their dresses. We stood for a long time watching them before we were interrupted.

"Can I help you?" the saleswoman asked as she quickly surveyed us. There was a cautious edge to her voice as she politely continued, "Do you have an appointment?"

Mena ignored her tone. "We're looking for a wedding dress. Our friend Shari is getting married and needs a gorgeous gown. We didn't make an appointment, but as we walked by the store, we saw your amazing display and wanted to see what you offered. Is it possible for us to get an appointment? Or can we just look at the gowns?"

The saleswoman's face lit up as she nodded. "Today is your lucky day. We've just had a last-minute cancellation and can fit her in right now. If you have the time, I'll be happy to accommodate you."

Mena pointed to Shari. "Yes, we do. Here is our bride-to-be. We want her to look stunning on her day."

Shari was now beaming like a newly engaged woman.

"Hi, I'm Irene," the saleswoman greeted her. "It's great to meet all of you. I want to reassure you that I've been dressing brides for decades, and I always know what'll make them look spectacular. By the way, Shari, I love your hair; not many women can carry it off. I have a dress in mind that has a bit of an edge, but it will still give you a bridal glow. Let's get you in a dress."

Like a dog blindly walking behind its owner, Shari obediently followed her through a door. Just before Irene left the room, she looked back at Mena and me and confidently added, "When she returns, she'll be in her perfect bridal dress."

Mena and I were now in a room filled with beautiful gowns and glittering jewellery. I looked at Mena, and she winked mischievously at me; I quickly suppressed my desire to giggle and reveal our ruse. While waiting for Shari, I browsed around, looking at the beautiful, ornate gowns: intricate pieces of artwork designed to make a woman believe she is a princess for a day.

"They're gorgeous," Mena cooed, "and so much more beautiful than when I got married. Maybe I should get Blair to renew our vows, although I know he'd think it's foolish."

I didn't reply.

"Hey, are you okay, Nicole?" she asked, after noticing that I was silent and not responding to her. "Is this bothering you?" Her voice suddenly rose with alarm. "Oh no,

I forgot. Oh shit, how could I be so selfish? I'm so sorry. I didn't think this through."

There was a lump in my throat. I couldn't talk. The events of the past couple of weeks hit me, knocking me over like a bowling ball hitting pins; I grabbed my stomach and keeled over. A saleswoman quickly came to me.

"Don't worry," Mena said as she shooed her away. "She's just so excited for our friend. Don't worry. She'll be okay."

"I get faint sometimes," I lied, hoping that I reassured the saleswoman, who was casting very concerned glances my way.

We got together today because I needed to talk with my friends. I wanted Shari to make me laugh with her outrageous comments, and I needed to listen to Mena's rational analysis putting my world into perspective.

Two months ago, I arrived home from work and discovered my husband, Powell, was no longer living with me. Before this realization, I took off my shoes and carefully stored them in their special cupboard. I then undressed and blindly put my hand into the closet to hang my suit expecting to war for a space, but my hand easily slid into the usually overstuffed closet. Shocked to feel the space, I instinctively thought that I'd been robbed, and I panicked. I quickly opened the closet doors, and to my amazement, there were dozens of empty hangers dangling on the rod. Just as I was about to grab the phone and dial 911, I noticed that only my husband's clothes were missing. I stopped moving, and everything in the room seemed to stand still. I remember going over to Powell's chest of drawers and discovering they were also empty. In a daze, I sat down on the bed we'd shared and quietly acknowledged that my husband had left me. There was no note or words explaining his departure. I remember sitting in shock and thinking, "How could this be? What should I do? How do I tell the kids?" I kept asking myself these questions over and over, but I couldn't find any answers. I must have sat there for quite a while because the next thing that I remember was the loud knock on my bedroom door and my son's loud voice.

"Mom, what's taking you so long?" Dustin yelled. "What are you doing in there? I'm hungry. We're hungry. When are we going to eat dinner?"

In that brief second, I stopped thinking about Powell and became a mother. Fearlessly, I threw on some sweats and went to the kitchen. I don't know how I remained calm, but I did. I quickly whipped up a scrumptious meal for my two children, and they surprised me by asking for seconds. That night, my teenagers were effluent with chatter as they told me about their day and even shared a few jokes. It was their voices that made me forget about the empty closet in my bedroom. On that evening, instead of rushing off to play video games as they usually did, they stayed with me, and we lounged at the dinner table laughing and talking for well over an hour.

When I was finally alone, my head was bombarded with many thoughts. Powell's leaving wasn't a total surprise, but how he did it shocked me. A woman shouldn't have to come home to an empty closet after being married to a man for over fifteen years. There should be a more civilized way to deal with a departure; my husband knew I was not one for yelling or theatrics. I'd never raised my voice at him even though he'd recently begun having an affair, and this woman wasn't his first indiscretion. Maybe a part of me knew that one day he'd find another bed that appeared cozier. Or maybe he just wasn't comfortable standing next to a woman who towered over him. I should have known something was up this morning when he pulled me to him.

He whispered seductively into my ear, "Nicole, I miss the feel of you...."

I stopped him; I didn't need to hear any more. My voice was calm, but he could hear my ire. "I wish I felt the same way you do, but I don't."

Then I got out of the bed. It'd been many months since we'd touched, and I didn't really care to be intimate with him. I now wondered if he wanted one last ride for his record books.

In my emotional state, I desperately needed someone to talk to and called Mena.

As soon as I heard her voice, I blurted, "Mena, I can't believe the amount of clothes that Powell owns."

She quickly replied, "You know men never like to admit that they love clothes as much as women do. I swear, I'm thinking about converting the extra bedroom into a walk-in closet because we need the space for all of Blair's things."

"Well, I can assure you that Powell took up too much

room in our closet," I interrupted. "It's now so empty that I can finally see what I own."

"What's up? Did you get finally get fed up and burn all of his stuff? You know if I was in your situation, there would have been a bonfire that'd be worthy of at least two or three fire trucks."

"No, I didn't need to do that. Powell emptied all his clothes from the closet."

"Hey, slow down, Nicole. What's going on? Are you saying he left you?"

"Yes, I think so. Everything that he owns is gone."

"Shit, you must be in shock. Are you okay? Do you need me to come over?" Mena asked in a very concerned tone.

"No, you don't need to come over."

"Are you sure? I don't want you to do something foolish."

"What can I do? Beg him to come back? Hell no. The truth is I'm doing better than I thought I would. I guess a part of me always knew this day could come. Maybe it hasn't hit me." I was quiet for a moment before I blurted out, "What do I say to the kids? How do I tell them that their father isn't coming home?"

"Slow down, Nicole. Take a deep breath. Are you sure he didn't leave a note?"

"Yes, I'm sure. I looked all over the room. There is nothing, nada. I've even texted him and called him, but no response. When he doesn't want to deal with something, he ignores it. I know his ways. He wants me to tell the kids that he's not coming home. This is so typical of him—let Nicole clean up the mess I made. What do I do?"

"As a counsellor, I often tell my patients to—"

"I'm not saying anything to them."

"What do you mean? Nicole, you can't run from this."

"Mena, for all these years, you've seen me lie and cover up his actions. I took care of everything by making excuse after excuse when he was late for a dinner party or forgot my birthday. Do you know how tiring that gets? It's fucking draining. This is what I think: I wasn't the one who walked out of the house—Powell did. So why do I need to say anything? For all I know he could have decided to dry clean all his clothes. I can't read his mind. If he is gone, he will have to tell the kids 'cause I'm not doing it. Fuck it. He's the man; let him act like one."

"If more of my patients thought like you, I wouldn't have a job." Mena chuckled for a moment before getting serious. "To be honest, I agree with you. And I'm not speaking as your therapist; I'm your girlfriend. This is what I think: you've been doing everything and making excuses for him for too damn long. Let him do what he's supposed to do."

I decided to just continue my life as a mother, friend, and a marketing manager working for a thriving importing company and not focus on Powell. Over the next few days, I maintained my routine of waking early, readying the kids for school, and then going to work, where I managed the production of brochures and met clients who'd stare incredulously at my five-eleven frame.

Although I'm not one for attention, I genuinely enjoy being in a crowd and knowing that I'll tower above everyone. My height is further bolstered by my love affair with high-heeled shoes, and I regularly stand well over six feet. I was a teenager when the world was shocked by Imelda Marcos's shoe collection. Back then she was reviled and despised for her lavish spending. I was silent whenever I heard someone make a disparaging comment about her extravagance. The truth is I was just plain jealous because she owned a pair of shoes to match every outfit and future ensembles. Although I'll never have as many shoes as Imelda, my collection is my pride, and each pair is lovingly stored in a specially designed wardrobe.

I spent the rest of the week rearranging the space in the closet and was pleased with the result because there was lots more room for my belongings. And I even began to think that I should ask Shari for her professional assistance so that I could buy new clothes to fill up the space.

Shari is a wardrobe consultant who transforms even the dowdiest woman into a femme fatale with her keen eye for style. Her client list includes a number of very powerful women in the city, and she drives in her bright yellow car from one end of Toronto to the other dressing them. Shari is a single mother with an artistic daughter who inherited her mother's style sense. When you see them together, it's like watching two seamless generations of fashionistas. Shari is truly my nuttiest friend. She doesn't believe in rules and totally deplores convention in all aspects of her life, from her clothing to her career. Every time I see her, she has a new hair colour. One week her short hair is platinum blonde, and another week she is sporting black hair with purple highlights; somehow her outfits always match her hairstyle. If you ask her, "Why do you change your hair colour so frequently?" She'll smile mischievously and say, "'Cause I can."

As I looked at my wardrobe, I am thankful to have her as a friend and am comforted knowing that she'd gladly help me.

I didn't say anything to the kids about Powell because I wasn't sure what was going on. He hadn't responded to any of my telephone or text messages. To be honest, I became more relaxed. With each passing day, I was more appreciative of my children, and I found myself freely laughing with them.

After he was gone a week, my cellphone rang. When I saw it was Powell's number, I reluctantly answered the call. His deep voice was on the next end of the line. "Hey, Nicole, it's Powell."

"Yes, I know your voice."

"How are the kids taking things? I shouldn't have left so abruptly. I should have explained. It's just that I needed some space and didn't know how to tell you. I'm worried about them. How have they taken my leaving?"

"I didn't mention anything to them."

"What? Are you telling me that my children haven't noticed that I'm not home and you didn't say anything?"

"They haven't asked about you. I guess they assumed you were away on a business trip and forgot to mention it because you're gone so much. And I didn't say anything because you never told me you'd left. I wasn't sure if you'd decided to dry clean all of your clothes."

"Nicole, what if something happened to me? Weren't you concerned even a little bit?"

"Powell, I know your bullshit ways, so don't bother using them. Stop being foolish and acting like an ass. You left me and the children and weren't man enough to say anything. As usual, you just thought I'd clean up the mess 'cause I always do. I have news for you. This time I'm not doing it. The only thing left between us will be decided in the courts."

Powell was silent. He didn't reply, but I knew he was seething with anger and was probably wondering if the woman on the line was really me. Then I heard a click; he was no longer on the phone. Shortly after we spoke, Powell was fiddling with his keys in the front door, and then he entered the house. I didn't go to meet him. If he needed to talk with me, he knew where I was. He stayed for around twenty minutes, then I heard the front door open and close. He was gone again. Before I could leave my room, I heard my kids running in the hallway. They clambered onto my bed. The space felt comfortably crowded. My son, who was already taller than his father, moved closer and threw his arms around me.

"We're fine, Mom," he said. "We're fine being with just you."

Shari glided into the room in a shimmering white gown. In that moment, I forgot everything.

"You're a princess," I gushed.

I was caught up in my friend's fantasy. I was exuberant and wowed by the sight of her in this fabulous gown. With Shari standing before me, in a gown fit for a queen, I felt my clock reversing; I was now a young woman in my twenties instead of a woman in her late thirties. And I forgot that Mena was married, I was going through a messy divorce with a man who was literally trying to take half of everything, and Shari hardly dated men. I was not the only person caught up in the magic of the moment. It was also on Mena's and Shari's faces. Everything was forgotten; life was beautiful. We were overjoyed with happiness.

After Shari left the room, Mena and I stared at each other, breathless and excited. The air felt light and full of magic, and we were beaming as we talked about how beautiful Shari looked in the dress.

As soon as we left the boutique, I screamed, "That was amazing! I forgot about all of my problems. And I even forgot that Powell thinks he has a right to half of the sheets on the kids' beds."

Then Mena added, "I keep telling you to light a bonfire. Then he'll have to fight for the embers."

Shari just looked at us with a big smile. "That was so fucking awesome. It made me want to be a bride."

Mena looked sheepish as she replied, "Then you'll have to sleep with a man."

And we all laughed. Shari's sex life is utterly and totally

fascinating. Mena and I think she has a strange hormonal cycle that awakens after long periods of dormancy. Like clockwork every five years, there is an attractive man on her arm and she is genuinely passionate for him. From her glow, there's no doubt that she's having hot, passionate sex. However, after around six months, she confides in Mena and me that he complains that her hairstyle is too crazy, and we know the clock has begun to tick on the relationship. The end is always the same: finally fed up with his criticism, she looks him directly in the eye. "Okay, I've had enough. I like my hair, and I don't care if you do. That's why you're no longer needed in my life."

When I got home after the dress-up event, I sat in my room and thought that I could get more space in my closet because there was a box that didn't need to be there. That's when I pulled it out. Without thinking, I opened the box where I had stored my wedding dress. I looked at the ornate monstrosity and wondered why I'd worn a dress that I didn't like. I impulsively decided to try on the dress, forgetting it was two sizes too small for me. Maybe I was thinking that I'd look as wonderful as Shari. Once I got the dress over my head, it was stuck. There I was, twisting and turning with my hands splayed high in the air, trying to get it on. I pushed and pulled, but it wouldn't budge. And as I tried to force it on, I heard a loud rip. The dress now had a large tear down the side, and my skin was pushing through the rip. I chuckled as I remembered I wasn't a size six anymore and that over fifteen years ago I walked down the aisle in flat shoes because Powell didn't want me to tower over him. Then I spoke out loud, "Nicole, you should have known better than to walk down the aisle in a pair of ugly shoes and wear this monstrosity."

I, somehow, got out of the dress and put my clothes back on. I went to the kitchen and grabbed a large green plastic bag and stuffed my wedding gown into it. A few days later, I was late for work because I wanted to watch the sanitation workers cart the dress away. I was really satisfied when I saw them throw it into the back of the truck and it got lost in a heap of smelly garbage, discarded like a rotten banana.

Two weeks later, Shari called Mena and me in a panic. One of her biggest clients was leaving town and wouldn't need her services anymore. She desperately needed a distraction because she was going insane trying to figure out how to afford tuition for her daughter's private school. That's when Mena suggested, "Hey, let's go wedding dress shopping again. If it helped Nicole forget about her divorce, I think it might clear your head."

This time, we went to a boutique on Queen Street. The interior wasn't as plush and glamorous as the Danforth shop, but the experience was the same. Once again, Shari donned a beautiful gown, and we were lost in the magic of the moment. We were hooked and knew this remedy was better than chocolate. And that's how trying on wedding dresses became our feel-good ritual.

It was not something we did every week, but we indulged in this fantasy on a regular basis. With Shari wearing a beautiful gown, we forgot that a child was failing school or a business deal didn't go as planned or some other blip in life happened. Each time Shari donned a dress and pretended she was a bride-to-be, we'd always experience that same rush of bliss and joy. All of our problems were forgotten. We weren't harming anyone, and we were truly thankful that we lived in a large city where we could hide our strange addiction by going to different bridal salons in Toronto.

Today is different. Over five years have passed since my friends and I began this ritual, and my life has changed dramatically. My friends and wedding dresses have helped me weather a divorce, comforted me as my children left for university, and helped me manoeuvre a new relationship.

I am in a lighthearted mood. I don't care that we now have to drive over an hour to find a boutique in the suburbs because we've visited every wedding shop in the city. In my cheerful state, I look at my friends and announce, "I want to wear a dress this time. Can I be the one to try it on?"

There is silence in the car.

"Hey, what bought this on? Did Jerome propose?" Mena asks.

"No. I just want to do this."

Shari shakes her head. "I'm sorry, but there has to be

something behind this request. If I remember correctly, you don't like the spotlight."

"I just want to wear one. Can't we leave it at that?"

"Fair enough," Mena replies. "I know there's more behind your request, but I'll leave it for now. It'd be great to see you in a dress for a change. Shari, you're always gorgeous, but I'd love to see Nicole in a gown. With her statuesque frame, I think she'll do it justice. And don't worry. I'm never going to ask to wear one; I don't plan on jinxing my marriage."

"Thanks for understanding, and look." I point to a bag. "I even bought a pair of shoes to try on with the dress. You know me and my shoes."

"Now I know we can't say no," Shari adds.

And that's how I am the one whom Mena points to when she says to the saleswoman, "We've made an appointment for our friend Nicole to try on dresses."

The woman looks knowingly at me. "Is this your second wedding?"

I nod.

"Congratulations!" She smiles. "Sometimes the first time is a test. But it's so wonderful that you've met someone to love again."

I can't find any words. She asks, "Do you have a budget?"

Finally, I find my voice. "Yes, around five thousand dollars." This will be my fantasy wedding, and I can do whatever I want. "However, whatever dress I choose, it must complement my shoes."

I pull out my pair of white lace high heels. "I couldn't do this the first time around because my ex wasn't very tall, but this time my fiancé is taller than me and I'm doing it my way."

The consultant grins knowingly. "You are a shoe woman, and what a fantastic pair!" She softly touches them and adds, "And most importantly, you found a man who complements you. Don't worry. I'll make sure your dress lets these shine."

I don't speak, as I'm fearful that if I say too much, I'll give away the ruse. I leave my dress choice in the hands of this capable woman who has been dressing brides for decades. She quickly sizes up every woman who walks into the boutique and knows what will work on their frame. She is adept at disguising thick waists and hanging bellies. And when she looks at me, she doesn't see a woman tired from yelling at her teenage children about cleaning their rooms or doing their homework. What she sees is my hope for a partner who will dance with me even if there is no music playing. She wants to send me to this mate, dressed in a gown that will make him smile for the rest of his life.

"When did you know he was the one?" she asks as she dresses me.

I couldn't tell her that I knew he was special when I stood next to him. Although I was wearing two-inch heels, he was still taller than me. He looked at me and nodded. "Wow, aren't you perfectly divine." The first time he made love to me, he felt my unease. My body was not that of a young woman, and my stomach had lost its flatness. As I looked uncomfortably at my bulging tummy, he caressed it, reminding me that it was still an erogenous zone. I saw his eyes held desire.

"I love your body," he whispered. "It's so perfectly wonderful. I know I'll never get enough of you."

At that moment, I realized he saw me as perfection, and I kissed him with total surrender as he pulled me to him.

Once the dress is on, the saleswoman says, "You can turn around and see yourself."

I shake my head. "No, not yet. I want my friends to see me before I look."

Their eyes tell me the dress is meant for me. I turn around and look in the mirror. I am no longer a middle-aged, divorced woman; I have transformed into a bride-to-be, filled with the joy of love. I stick out my legs to see that the dress works with my shoes. Everything is perfect; yes, it's better the second time around. In that moment, wearing that beautiful dress, I feel a sense of hope, and I also smile sweetly as I remember Jerome's words this morning.

Shari screams, "You look stunning! Better than your first wedding. I didn't think it was possible."

Mena is quiet for a moment and then quietly states, "I'd marry you in that."

The sales clerk looks confident, assured of her sale. But there is no wedding. We are here for the wrong reason: three girlfriends having fun.

"What do you think?" she eagerly asks.

I hesitate. "It's great, but I'm not ready to make a commitment. I want to think about this some more."

The room feels cold as she peels the dress off me. She is thinking about her lost sale—I feel deceptive and wish there is a way to stop this. I wonder how Shari tries on dresses on a regular basis. My clothes feel drab and inconsequential once I have them on. I can't look the saleswoman in the eye. And I quickly leave the boutique with my girlfriends.

We are all silent as we get into the car.

"Shari, how do you do it? I felt horrible pretending. How do you do it?" I blurt out.

"Nicole, each time I try it on, I believe. Maybe there is a man out there who thinks my hair is absolutely divine. In the meantime, I'm just doing lots of window-shopping. You know me. If I was really getting married, I'd probably try on at least a hundred gowns."

Mena interrupts, "It'll be more like two hundred, and we'd probably have to make a trip to New York City or something crazy like that."

"Okay, I know that I'd go crazy if it ever happened. But, Nicole, I don't get why you did what you did today. Why did you put on that dress?"

I tell them that as I dressed this morning, I looked at Jerome's body sleeping in my bed. I tried not to wake him as I was leaving, but he stirred and pulled me close to him when I went to give him a quick peck on the cheek. We'd successfully passed the dreaded six-month hurdle, and now we were closing in on our one-year anniversary. When he asked me about my plans for the day, I pretended to shrug them off, not wanting to share this side of my life with him.

"I'm just getting together with the girls for some estrogen time."

"When I get together with the boys, it's about sports and more sports. Okay, I'm lying a bit; we also talk about women."

"We are so different. I never even mention your name," I teasingly replied. "Okay, that's not the truth, but we go shopping. You know how women love to shop."

"Yeah, but in all the times that you've gone out with them, I've never seen you come home with anything."

"Guilty. It's just that I haven't seen anything that I really like when I'm with them. You've met my friends before. Why are you being so inquisitive? Normally, you don't ask any questions."

"You're acting different, like you're hiding something. I'm not sure what it is. In fact, I've heard you whispering with your friends all week, and I know you are planning something."

I didn't reply.

"Hey, what secret event are you and your friends planning? Are you running off with some next guy?"

"No, of course not!" I see him look at me, his eyes pleading for the truth, and I know I have to confess. "You'll laugh if I tell you, so I don't want to say anything. It's a silly thing that we do every now and then."

"What is it?"

"We try on wedding dresses."

"What?"

"You heard me. We try on wedding dresses."

"I really did hear right."

"Yes, I know it's crazy, but that's what we do."

"Why would you do something like that? And how many have you tried on?"

"I've never tried one on. Shari loves doing it. And Mena refuses to try on a dress, as she thinks it'll jinx her happiness. I know it's silly and stupid. But we have so much fun when we do, it's like we forget our problems."

Jerome was silent for a long time. Then he looked serious as he stared into my eyes. "Do you think you'll marry again?"

I was quiet now, fearful of answering the question, knowing that the wrong word could end this wonderful relationship.

He saw my hesitation and continued, "Be honest, Nicole. I'll speak first since I brought this up. I'd like to remarry. I want to be with someone who wants to walk down the road with me. And I know when I'm with you that we're a real good feeling. Do you think we have that kind of staying power?"

"Wow, I didn't expect this. And, yes, I like us and I want to believe it can always be like this."

"The truth is I'd like one year to be two years and then three years. I'd love this to keep going on."

"So do I. Hey, are you proposing?"

"Not yet. But you go and enjoy your day, and I won't ask you about it again."

My friends are quiet. Mena speaks first. "Now I know why you shone in that dress. You were so different compared to Shari. You were wearing it because you knew that one day it just might be you in a dress."

Shari is silent, but then she shocks us with her words. "I never told you that I was married before."

Mena and I look at her in utter surprise. I say, "Are you serious? We've known you for nearly twenty years and you've never said anything."

"It was a short marriage, a youthful dalliance."

"There is nothing called a quick marriage—only celebrities make those idiotic decisions," Mena replies.

"Hey, then I have some star power in me. I was a wild child. Hell, I'm still a little nutty. Wouldn't you expect this from me?"

Mena turns to her. "Yes, I can see you doing something like that."

Shari was nineteen when she and her boyfriend went to Las Vegas for a weekend. She giggles. "And at that time, I had sex more than once every five years. Believe it or not, we made love at least twice a day."

In their youthful impetuousness and drunken state, they impulsively decided to get married. Once they started living together, Shari hated his untidiness. He threw his underwear on the ground and left it for her to pick up. Her new husband also avoided housework and didn't know how to wash dishes. He claimed that he needed to find the right instructor to school him in the art of cleanliness. However, whenever Shari tried to show how to clean up, he'd leave their home. Each day, he disappeared as soon as he had his bath, and she was left with his trail of dirty clothes on the floor and a sink full of dishes. She thought he only saw her as his personal maid, and this reality check made her love wane. Shari became more assertive and told him that he must do his part around the house, and he decided that the best way to deal with her was to become close with their neighbour. He took to spending time in her bed while Shari made the house spotless. That's why Shari cleaned up the house, called a locksmith, changed the lock, and found herself a lawyer.

"I never married again. And I can't boast that I've had great relationships. I don't know if it's my lack of a sex drive, my hairstyle, or my independent spirit." She is silent before continuing. "But the fashionista in me has one really big regret—I didn't wear one of these extravagant gowns."

"It could happen. You could meet someone. Nicole did," Mena quietly adds.

"I don't really care if it happens or doesn't," Shari quickly replies. "But I really enjoy putting on those dresses. Perhaps I'll just have a wedding dress party theme. I'll tell my married friends to take their old dress out of the box and come dressed as a bride. And my unmarried compatriots will have a chance to wear a gown and feel like a bride."

"I'll definitely be there, but I'm not wearing mine, since I've already thrown it away," I remind them.

"Then we'll definitely have to go dress hunting for you and me," Shari responds.

"Hey, I'm not wearing that monstrosity that I got married in again," Mena announces.

"We'll all go shopping together," Shari says. "But we have a problem because I think we've visited every shop in the city. That means we'll have to go to New York for a weekend."

I ask, "Then what will we do in Toronto for fun?"

Mena chuckles. "Well, I think we're at the age when we can go shopping just for the hell of it. Maybe we'll try on lots of shoes."

Mena and Shari are my friends. We talk about everything, from mundane tasks like getting stains out of clothes to our fears about our children's future. I can't imagine my life without these two women. No matter if I have a good or bad day, I just have to pick up the phone and they always know what to say or do to make me feel good.